HOMETOWN HEARTS

A Man to Rely On

CINDI MYERS

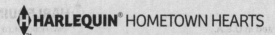

If you purchased this book without a cover you should be aware that this book is stolen property. It was reported as "unsold and destroyed" to the publisher, and neither the author nor the publisher has received any payment for this "stripped book."

ISBN-13: 978-0-373-21483-9

A Man to Rely On

Copyright © 2009 by Cynthia Myers

HARLEQUIN® HOMETOWN HEARTS

Recycling programs
for this product may
not exist in your area.

ISBN-13: 978-0-373-21483-9

A Man to Rely On

HARLEQUIN®

www.Harlequin.com

Printed in U.S.A.

Cindi Myers is the author of more than fifty novels. When she's not crafting new romance plots, she enjoys skiing, gardening, cooking, crafting and daydreaming. A lover of small-town life, she lives with her husband and two spoiled dogs in the Colorado mountains.

For Pam,
who loved this story in all its incarnations.

Prologue

Cedar Switch, Texas, 1988

"Did you hear? She's going to do it. She's really going to do it."

"Do what?" Scott Redmond struggled to keep up with his friend, Sam Waite, as they splashed through the muddy shallows above the swimming hole in the Brazos River. It was after noon on a Thursday in August, and the river was the temperature of bath water. The air smelled of weeds and mud and the beachy scent of Coppertone oil.

He lunged through the thigh-high water. At fourteen, Sam was a year older and a head taller. His legs were longer too, and he moved faster in the water.

Scott scrambled for purchase on the slick river bottom. With a loud splash, he fell, and came up sputtering, muddy water filling his eyes and nose. Sam didn't even notice, he was so intent on reaching the bridge. Around him, other kids were making their way upstream toward the bridge too. In local swimming hole hierarchy, the bridge was the territory of older kids, who took turns daring each other to leap from the creosote posts that supported the guardrail beside the highway.

"What's going on?" Scott asked, as he stood and slicked his hair back out of his eyes.

"Marisol Luna is gonna jump off the bridge," a boy Scott's age said.

"So?" Kids did it all the time. He hadn't yet, but he probably would soon. At least by the time he was in high school.

"She's gonna do it *naked*!" The other boy's eyes lit up with a wicked gleam. "C'mon. You don't want to miss this."

The chance to see a female naked in broad daylight was not something that happened very often in the lives of most thirteen-year-olds in Cedar Switch, Texas. Inspired by this rare prospect, Scott floundered through the water again, determined not to miss the spectacle.

When he joined the crowd gathered beneath the high concrete span, he could see the group of older kids on the bridge. Danny Westover was the high school football team's quarterback. His sometimes-girlfriend, Jessica Freeman, was there, along with half a dozen other high school boys and girls. And in front of them all was a girl Scott thought he had seen around town before: a Mexican girl with curly black hair that hung past her shoulders. She wore a modest one-piece tank suit, red with black roses printed on it.

"That's her. That's Marisol," Sam said, pointing.

Scott nodded. "I know. What makes you think she's gonna jump?" He couldn't even say the part about her being naked. It was too impossible to imagine.

"Jessica dared her. She said if Marisol thought she was such hot stuff, she ought to let them all see."

"And she said yes?" The girls he knew got mad if you said something about the strap of their training bras showing. He couldn't imagine one of them voluntarily taking her clothes off in broad daylight before God and everybody.

A hush fell over the crowd in the water as Marisol stepped up onto the flat top of the thick post that supported part of the guardrail. She didn't look at any of them. Instead, she stared out across the water. Scott held his breath, awed by the expression on her face. She wasn't that much older than him—maybe fifteen or sixteen. But she looked so determined. Not scared at all. He'd seen girls jump before—with their swimsuits on—and every one of them had looked like she was about to cry before she dove into the water.

But Marisol Luna looked calm, as if she was waiting to cross the street in front of the school.

"Take it off! Take it off!" Someone started the chant and others picked it up, until it was a deafening chorus, echoing off the water.

Scott remained silent, watching the girl on the post. She glanced down at the water, and in that moment, her expression changed. She looked angry, he decided. Was she angry at Jessica and her friends for taunting her? Or at all of them for watching?

He ducked his head, feeling ashamed, then quickly brought it up again, unable to resist seeing her fulfill the dare. He looked at her again, and this time, he saw hurt alongside the anger. He felt the hurt in his own chest, but still could not turn away.

She brought one hand to the strap of her suit, and a half smile formed on her lips. She reached back and undid the strap slowly, then let it fall down across her still-covered breasts, taunting them.

"Take it off! Take it off!" The volume of the chant increased.

The same amused expression fixed on her face, she grabbed the top of the suit with both hands and shoved it down, then quickly stepped out of it.

The chant faded away in the heavy, hot air. Scott stared at the girl, his heart pounding painfully in his chest. She had small round breasts, tipped with dark brown nipples, a small waist and round hips. He could see the tuft of dark brown hair between her legs, and felt a stiffness between his own legs. He stifled a groan and sank deeper into the water, not daring to take his eyes from her for a moment.

She raised her hands over her head and held the pose for what seemed like a full minute. No one said anything. Scott could hear the water slapping against the concrete pilings of the bridge, and the buzzing of dragonflies that hovered on the river's surface, and his own frantic pulse throbbing in his ears.

Then she dove, her legs and arms folded together in a perfect jackknife, cleaving the water like a bullet.

The mournful keening of a siren broke the stillness, and a sheriff's car came to a halt on the bridge. A deputy climbed out of the car, his uniform shirt plastered to his back by sweat. "What are you kids doing?" he bellowed. "Y'all know you're not supposed to dive off here."

They scattered then, swimming or running away from the site. When Scott looked back, the deputy was holding up Marisol's swimsuit and talking with Jessica and Danny. He dropped his gaze to the water, but Marisol was nowhere in sight. Scott froze, half sick with fear. What if she'd drowned?

Then he saw her, farther down the bank, half-hidden in the salt cedars that grew beside the river. She was picking her way through the shallows, moving away from the bridge, as graceful as a mermaid, and as naked as the day she was born. Scott stared until he couldn't see her anymore, then he reluctantly made his way home.

That night, and many night afterwards, he dreamed of Marisol, standing on the bridge. Of the beauty of her body, and the defiance and pain that shone from her eyes. In his dreams, he wanted more than anything to comfort her, but she was unreachable, someone he could only long for from afar.

Chapter One

Cedar Switch, Texas, 2008

Marisol Luna once said she would never come back to Cedar Switch, Texas, except to dance on the graves of all those who had scorned her. The image pleased her, of whirling and tapping and kicking and leaping past the stolid tombstones of the men and women who had looked down their noses at her. Her steps would reverberate down to where they lay unmoving in their coffins, and reduce the soil over them to dust.

As far as she knew, most of those people were still alive. Alive and well enough to see her come home with her head ducked in shame.

She'd disappoint them in that respect at least. Of all the emotions that had dogged her in the past nightmare of a year, shame had not been one of them. She had done nothing wrong. A judge and a jury had said so—though her enemies would never believe it.

Correction. She had done one thing wrong. She'd made the mistake of falling in love with a man who kept more secrets than the CIA. Her hands tightened on the steering wheel as she thought of her late husband. Lamar Dixon, star center for the Houston Rockets, the highest paid player in the history of professional basketball, had been a liar and a cheat and a gambler who lost more than he could ever afford to repay. In the end, it had cost him his life, and it had almost cost Marisol hers.

But that was over now. She was making a fresh start. Cedar Switch was only the first stop in her new life. She'd stay long enough to sell the house her mother had left her, then take that money and head to a place where no one had heard of Lamar Dixon or his infamous widow.

Marisol glanced toward the passenger seat. Her fourteen-year-old daughter, Antonia— Toni—had her eyes closed, bobbing her head in time to some hip-hop tune on her iPod.

Oblivious to her mother. Toni had Marisol's light brown skin and wide mouth, and her father's strong chin and thick, unruly hair, which she wore in long braids gathered with a clip at the nape of her neck. She'd been a pretty child and would be a beautiful woman, if Marisol could only manage to see her through these turbulent teen years.

As if feeling her mother's gaze on her, Toni jerked the earbuds of the iPod from her ears. "I can't believe you're moving me all the way to East Podunk," she said, picking up the argument that had raged between mother and daughter for days. "I don't know why we couldn't stay in Houston."

"Did you really want to spend the rest of your life barricaded in your house, dodging reporters?"

Toni stuck out her lower lip and twined the cord of the iPod between her fingers. "They would have gone away, eventually."

"Maybe. But the truth of the matter is, we couldn't afford to stay in Houston any longer," Marisol said. "I spent pretty much everything we had on lawyers."

Toni's eyes widened. "Do you mean we're poor?"

Marisol's idea of poor and her daughter's

were probably several decimal places apart, but Marisol understood that to Toni their present reduced circumstances might seem dire. She had some money set aside—enough to pay for Toni's education. But she was determined not to touch it. "We're not rich," she said. "And I'll have to get a job. But you don't need to worry about having enough to eat or a roof over your head."

Toni slumped back in the seat with a sigh. "I just wish we could go home," she moaned.

Me too, Marisol thought. But the house in River Oaks, the platinum credit cards, the exclusive clubs and the luxury vacations had disappeared with Lamar's death. All she had left was her car, a small savings account and the house she'd inherited from her mother. That house was her ticket to a new future, a less extravagant one for sure, but one in which she'd call her own shots. After her experience with Lamar, it would be a long time before she was so naive as to trust anyone else again.

A green city limits sign announced their arrival in Cedar Switch, Texas, population 9,016. Marisol turned her attention from her daughter as she guided the red Corvette down Main Street. She wished now she'd sold the car and bought something more conservative, but she'd told herself she could always trade it in later if things got really bad. Lamar had given her the vehicle for her last birthday; it was one happy memory to hold on to in spite of everything that had happened since then.

But the Corvette was definitely the kind of car that made people take a second look, and when folks in Cedar Switch realized who was in the car...

She took a deep breath and told herself to get over it. Why should anyone care if she was here now? Likely no one remembered what had happened all those years ago.

"What a dump," Toni said, scowling at the passing scenery.

"Actually, it looks better than it did when I was here last," Marisol said. In her memories, everything here was sepia-toned—the brown brick of the courthouse, the faded facades of storefronts and the yards of houses brown from winter's frosts or summer's drought. So it surprised her to recognize color all around her. Azaleas bloomed pink and lilac around the courthouse. New stores with bright striped awnings lined the streets.

She drove past the corner where the Dairy Freeze had once sat—now occupied by a bright yellow McDonald's—and turned onto a wide,

shady street. Her destination was halfway
down, on the right. She blinked rapidly, curs-
ing the tears that stung her eyes as she stared
at the familiar white brick ranch house, with
its narrow front porch and cracked concrete
drive. Even the mailbox was the same, the paint
faded over the years but still readable: Davies.

She pulled in front of the garage and shut
off the engine. "This is it?" Toni asked. "It's
so tiny."

Marisol laughed, a bitter attempt to avoid
bursting into tears. "It's little to you because
you're used to our huge house in Houston. But
when I was a little girl, this seemed like a really big house." Before Mercedes Luna had
married Harlan Davies, she and Marisol had
shared a one-bedroom apartment over a dry
cleaner's downtown. Marisol had stayed in
bigger hotel rooms than the place where she'd
spent the first eleven years of her life.

Toni shook her head, unimpressed by nostal-
gia, and shoved open her car door then climbed
out.

Marisol sighed and got out as well. She re-
frained from looking around as she headed up
the walk to the front door. The neighbors were
probably already getting cricks in their necks,
trying to see what was going on at the Davies'

house. The phone lines would be buzzing when they figured out who was back in town.

She dug in her purse for the key the lawyer had sent. Toni waited on the porch, slumped against the post, feigning boredom, though impatience radiated from her. No matter what she said, the girl was interested in this glimpse into her mother's past—a past Marisol had never found reason to share with her.

She took a deep breath, bracing herself against the onslaught of memory, then turned the key in the lock and pushed open the door.

It took a moment for her eyes to adjust to the dimness in the closed-up room, but in that time the scent of White Shoulders filled her. Her mother's perfume. One breath and it was as if Mercedes were there in person, urging her daughter to shut the door and come inside. To make herself at home.

She groped for the light switch. A single yellow bulb glowed feebly overhead, revealing furniture draped in old sheets, and the same red-and-black patterned rug that had been bought new when Marisol was eleven.

Toni gingerly lifted one sheet. "You really lived here?" she asked.

Marisol nodded. She had not really wanted to come here, but told herself she had no choice. Staying here until she could sell the place seemed like the safest bet for her and her daughter. And she couldn't deny a curiosity, a need to see what had become of this place she had left so long ago. An unvoiced hope that in death Mercedes might have left behind some clue as to what had really happened to tear them so irrevocably apart.

"I want to stay in your room," Toni said, interrupting her mother's reverie. Before Marisol could stop her, she hurried down the hall, opening doors as she went, looking in at the dusty furnishings of a guest room/home office, bathroom and finally, at the end of the hall, Marisol's girlhood room.

"Toni, no," Marisol called, but too late. Toni had already opened the door and stood just inside it, staring.

Marisol came up behind her and stared too, at the white single bed with its pink puffy comforter. The pink curtains, faded by the sun, still hung in the window, and the pink fluffy rug still lay by the bed.

She took Toni's shoulder and urged her gently over the threshold into the hall. "You don't want to stay here," she said. "We'll fix up the guest room for you."

"Why can't I stay here?" Toni whirled on

her, her face fixed in the stubborn pout Marisol recognized too well. "What's in there you don't want me to see?"

Marisol closed her eyes and breathed deeply through her nose—a technique she had read somewhere was calming, but she couldn't tell that it made any difference now. She still felt as if she'd swallowed broken glass, as if there was no move she could make that didn't hurt. "There's nothing special here to see," she said calmly, though a voice in her head screamed *Liar!* "It's just a house. You can look at it later. Let's unpack our things first."

Toni blocked her mother's passage down the hall, arms folded across her chest, mouth set in a stubborn scowl. Already she was taller than Marisol, having inherited her father's height. "What was the deal with you and your mother, anyway? How come I never met her? How come she didn't want you attending her funeral? Why do you always keep so many secrets?"

Not secrets, Marisol thought. *Just things no one needs to talk about anymore.* She wet her dry lips. "I didn't get along with her husband. She chose him over me." The truth, but only part of it.

"And that's it? You let something like that keep you apart for what—twenty years?"

"About that." She forced herself to look her daughter in the eye, to not flinch from that disdainful glare. It was so easy to judge at this age, when you were so sure of right and wrong. "I'm not proud of it. If I could go back and do things differently, I would. But I can't. So now I have to live with it."

Toni scowled at her, then pushed past, headed to the living room. Marisol followed her daughter and sank onto a sheet-covered sofa, her legs suddenly too weak to support her. Oh God, why had she come back here? True, she hadn't seen any other choice. But everything felt wrong. There were too many bad memories in these walls, too much hurt to have to deal with. She looked around the room, at the shrouded shapes that were like so many ghosts, taunting her.

Toni slumped in the chair opposite. "So what do we do now?" she asked.

Marisol took a deep breath. "We're going to do whatever we have to," she said. That was how she'd lived her life. She'd done tougher things to survive before. She could do this. She could do anything as long as she knew it was only temporary.

Scott Redmond leaned against the door to his father's office and watched his dad, attorney Jay

Redmond, shuffle through stacks of folders. "I need to pick up my dry cleaning," the old man muttered. "I know the claim slip is here somewhere."

"Just tell Mr. Lee you lost it," Scott said. "It's not as if he hasn't known you for years." That was one good thing about living in a small town for years—everyone knew everything about you.

And that was the worst thing about living in a small town as well. Mess up even once and no one ever forgot it. Make a habit of screw-ups and it could take years to rebuild a reputation, something Scott was finding out the hard way.

Two years ago he'd been the top-selling real estate agent in town, riding the tail end of a housing boom that had brought wealthy investors from Houston, three hours to the north, to buy up old homes or build new ones on vacant land for weekend retreats. Scott had wined and dined these high rollers and become something of a roller himself. He'd ended up with habits he couldn't afford and made some really stupid mistakes. Only his dad's influence and Scott's own remorse had kept him from serious trouble.

So here he was at thirty-four years old, starting over at the bottom. A one-man real estate office sharing space with his attorney father.

"Found it!" His father held a yellow slip of paper aloft triumphantly. "Now I won't have to defend Eddie Stucker wearing my golf clothes." He settled back in his worn leather desk chair. "Speaking of golf—how's Marcus Henry's latest project coming along?"

Scott almost smiled at this not-so-subtle maneuvering of the conversation to Henry's—and Scott's—latest triumph. Scott suspected heavy lobbying from Jay had led Cedar Switch's biggest developer to award Scott the exclusive listing for his most ambitious project to date—an upscale development centered around a Robert Trent Jones golf course, private lake, stables and green belt.

"The roads are going in this week and next," Scott said. "I've got some people coming from Houston this weekend to take a tour. Once the streets are in and the clubhouse starts going up, we expect to see a flurry of interest."

"Everything the man touches turns to gold," Jay said. "Getting in with him is one of the best things that could have happened to you. You'll give the other agencies around here a real run for their money. Before long this office won't be big enough for you. You'll have to have new space, hire associates…it'll be just like the old days."

The old days of only two years ago? "Not just like them," Scott said. "I'm done with life in the fast lane."

His father's expression sobered. "You're right," he said. "You shouldn't try to take on too much. Better to keep things manageable. You don't need the stress."

Scott resented the implication that he wasn't strong enough to handle whatever the job required. If he wanted a different kind of life now, it wasn't because he couldn't cope with more. He'd simply learned some things about himself and what was important to him now.

Others didn't see things that way, though. To them, he was Scott Redmond—Jay's boy who'd had such a bright future and thrown it all away.

Scott would probably spend the rest of his life paying for the recklessness of that one half year.

He was about to excuse himself, to walk to McDonald's and grab some lunch when the door opened and a woman entered. She was beautiful, with long dark curly hair, smooth, olive skin, a classic hourglass figure and an air of money and poise he associated with socialites from Dallas and Houston who spent weekends shopping in the "quaint" shops on the town square.

Jay rose to greet his visitor. "May I help you?"

"Mr. Redmond?" She flashed a dazzling smile. "I'm Marisol Luna."

But of course they had both recognized her by then, the beautiful face less strained, the clothes less severe than they had been in countless pictures splashed across the front pages of newspapers and filling their television screens each night. The Lamar Dixon murder trial had all the elements of riveting drama: the celebrity victim, the beautiful accused, wealth, glamor, sexual affairs, gambling and unsavory secrets. People chose sides, wagered bets on Marisol's guilt or innocence and read everything they could find about the case.

"Please sit down." Jay gestured to the chair before his desk. "What can I do for you? Ms. Luna? You've gone back to your maiden name?"

"I thought it best."

She sat, demurely crossing her legs at the ankles and smoothing her skirt down her thighs. Scott struggled not to stare at her.

"This is my son, Scott. You might remember him from school."

Scott stepped forward to shake her hand, a brief silken touch gone too soon. He was sure Marisol did not remember him, though he had never forgotten her. His heart beat faster, remembering that day on the bridge. She wouldn't have known him then, of course, but later, she had come to their house once. He'd been fourteen at the time, in awe of her sixteen-year-old beauty and her notoriety.

A notoriety she maintained years later, when the local papers were full of news of her marriage to basketball great Lamar Dixon. He'd seen Lamar on the basketball court once in Houston. Lamar had netted twenty-seven baskets in that game and hadn't even broken a sweat. The papers had reported his last contract at seventeen million, making him one of the highest paid stars in the NBA.

And of course the murder charge and trial had only added to her reputation.

"I'm sorry about your husband's passing," Jay said. "And about everything you've been through."

"Thank you." She folded her hands in her lap. She looked very…contained. Behind the outward polish, Scott sensed she was shaken by more than grief.

"How have you been?" Jay asked.

"I've been fine." Her voice was flat. Unemotional. The voice of someone concentrating on staying in control. Scott could feel the tension radiating from her, and she sat so rigidly he imagined she might shatter if touched.

Jay's response was to relax even more, leaning back in the chair, hands casually clasped on the desktop. He'd once told Scott that the best way to handle fearful or nervous clients was to ease the tension with small talk. "It's been a while since you've been back to Cedar Switch, hasn't it?" he said. "I imagine it's changed a lot since then."

"It's been a long time," she said. "To tell you the truth, I'm more surprised by how much has remained the same."

"Really?" Jay leaned forward. "Having lived here so long myself, it seems as if every other day some old building is being torn down and replaced by something new."

She shifted in her chair. "I guess what I mean is that, for me at least, the town has the same feeling it always did."

Scott and his father waited for her to elaborate on what that feeling might be, but when she did not, Scott wondered if she was waiting for him to leave. "I'll let you two talk in private," he said, moving toward the door.

"I don't mind if you stay." He felt a jolt when their eyes met, a shock of recognition that, even after all these years, this woman could stir him somewhere deep inside. He settled slowly into a chair a little ways from her and searched for something innocuous to say.

"Is your daughter with you?" Jay asked.

Scott vaguely recalled the mention in news reports of a teenage daughter.

"Yes. Antonia isn't too happy about being here in 'East Podunk' as she insists on calling it."

"I'll bet she's as pretty as her mother was at that age," Jay said.

Scott could see the girl Marisol had been so clearly in his mind's eye, exotically beautiful to a small-town boy like himself.

"Prettier, I hope. She's tall, like her father." Pride warmed her voice and softened her expression.

"You're staying at your mother's place?" Jay asked. "Your place now, of course."

"Yes. I appreciate your handling transferring the title and everything after she died," she said. "I obviously wasn't in a position to come down and handle it myself."

As Scott recalled, when Mercedes Luna had passed away, her only daughter had been confined to a cell in the Harris County Jail.

"I was happy to do it," Jay said. "And it's good to have you home."

Marisol looked uncomfortable with the word, Scott thought. Then again, why would a woman like her, used to the finest things in life and the social whirl of a big city, ever feel at home in a small house in a sleepy place like Cedar Switch?

"I plan to stay here for a little while," she said. "Until I can sell the house. That's what I came to see you about. I was hoping you could recommend a real estate agent. I'd like to list the house as soon as possible. I didn't know who else to ask."

Jay's smile broadened. "You came to the right place. Scott here is an excellent agent, and his office is right next door."

She looked at Scott again, her gaze lingering, and he had the impression he was being judged. Sized up. "That's very convenient," she said. "Do you think you can sell my mother's house?"

"I'll be happy to help you find a buyer," he said.

"Thank you." She looked away from him again, her hands knotted tightly in her lap, gaze focused somewhere above his father's desk. The silence went on so long he began to feel uneasy.

"Is there anything else I can help you with?" Jay asked.

She took a deep breath. "You've always been so kind to me," she said.

"I've always liked you very much." Jay's voice was gentle. He cleared his throat. "We all do."

Her eyes widened, as if in surprise, for half a second—such a fleeting expression Scott wasn't entirely sure he'd actually seen it. The unnaturally calm mask was back in its place. "I have some questions I hope you can answer," she said.

"I'll do my best." Jay relaxed in his chair again, while Scott continued to study the woman who sat a few feet away, unable to tear his eyes from her. The beauty he remembered had matured to something deeper, something more compelling even than the girl who had cast a spell over him.

"Why didn't my mother want me at her funeral?" she asked, her accusing tone startling after the long silence.

"There wasn't a funeral," Jay said. "She insisted on that. I suppose, given the circumstances, she thought it best."

Marisol laced her fingers together. "I had permission to come to town for a funeral," she said. "My lawyers even thought it would help gain sympathy for me."

When the media learned there was to be no funeral—that it had been her mother's last wishes that Marisol *not* return to Cedar Switch—the press had trumpeted the news for weeks. Marisol was so bad, her own mother had rejected her. Of course a woman like that would murder her husband.

Jay frowned. "I didn't know Mercedes well," he said. "But I don't think she even considered doing you any harm. I think she was simply a very private person who didn't want any fuss over her. She wanted everything taken care of so you wouldn't have to bother."

"And she told you to wait until after she was buried before you contacted me?"

"Yes. I tried to talk her out of the idea. I told her you would want to be contacted. She made me promise not to bother you."

"Was that the word she used? *Bother?*"

He nodded. "Yes. She said it would be better for everyone if all the details were out of the way and over with before you even knew she was gone. I couldn't convince her otherwise."

Marisol's shoulders sagged, and her fingers played with the strap of her purse, stroking the leather over and over. In that moment she seemed more vulnerable than she had since walking into the office. Scott fought the urge to put his arms around her. But the fact that he wanted so much to touch her kept him firmly in his chair. What he felt for the woman across from him went beyond sympathy for a client or compassion for an old friend. His feelings for Marisol were too mixed up with adolescent desire, unfulfilled fantasy and maybe even the fact that as an adult she was so much like the women who had attracted him during his high-flying days—polished, sophisticated women whose outer sleekness was a thin coating over an earthy sensuality. He couldn't separate all these facets of his attraction to Marisol in his mind, and therefore had no business laying a finger on her.

She stood suddenly, poised once more. She extended her hand to Jay. "Thank you for talking with me."

"If there's anything I can do, don't hesitate to ask."

"Thank you." She turned to Scott. "I'll want to sell the house as soon as possible."

"I can come out late today or tomorrow to look at it and draw up a listing agreement."

"Tomorrow would be best, thank you." She turned to leave. He stood and followed her, holding the door open for her. Then he moved to the window and watched her walk to a bright red Corvette that was parked at the curb. He smiled. He would have guessed the girl who stood naked on the bridge and the woman who held her head high and faced the television cameras head-on would drive a car like this. A car that dared everyone to watch her. As they always had.

As *he* always had.

Chapter Two

Marisol woke the next morning to golden light streaming through the yellow curtains in her mother's old bedroom. Lying there in a place she had never imagined she would find herself she felt the impotence of a person in a dream, unsure her legs would support her if she tried to rise. The grief she had fought for days battered at her, waves of memory threatening to drown her: her mother teaching her to make tortillas when Marisol was five years old, Mercedes's larger hands over her small ones, helping her to pat out the flat disks of dough; mother and daughter watching the movie *Grease* at a matinee at the Cedar Switch cinema, sharing a tub of buttery popcorn and pretending to swoon over John Travolta; the pink silky dress she wore to her mother's remarriage, and how much she'd cried when the newlyweds left her behind for their brief honeymoon.

Mercedes had told her she was gaining a father that day, but in truth Marisol had lost her mother to Harlan Davies. He had been a hard, possessive man, who had demanded Mercedes take his side in all disputes. Until finally he had dug a chasm between mother and daughter that could not be crossed, not even after his death.

If Marisol could have asked her mother one question now, it would be if she felt all she'd gained by marrying Davies had been worth all he had forced her to surrender.

She shut her eyes tightly and forced her mind from such thoughts. She had too much to do to indulge her grief. This morning she had to see about finding a job; the few thousand dollars left in her bank account after she'd paid the legal team and all their investigators, and settled the debts Lamar had left her with would not last long. And she absolutely would not touch Toni's college fund. Lamar's death had robbed his daughter of the advantages of wealth and privilege; Marisol would not deprive her of a first-class education as well.

Besides, working would keep Marisol occupied and out of the house until it sold and they could leave town for good.

What kind of job she had no idea. Years of attending charity balls, shopping and lunching with her friends had left her without any marketable skills. But she was smart. She could learn.

She'd spent the previous afternoon arguing with Toni, who had wanted to explore the town on her own. Marisol had refused to consider the idea, which had led to a shouting match, ending with Toni declaring, "I hate you!" and retreating to Marisol's old room, where she'd plugged in her iPod and refused to budge, even to eat.

How many times had Marisol acted out a similar scene with her own mother? If anything, she had been more unruly than Toni, sneaking out of the house at all hours of the day and night, purposely doing things she knew would enrage Harlan. Only now, from the perspective of an adult and a parent herself, could she understand how much her rebelliousness must have also hurt her mother.

She forced herself out of bed, made coffee,

then knocked on her daughter's door. Toni had insisted on moving into Marisol's bedroom. "Toni, are you up? I need to go out for a while."

"I'm up."

"There's cereal and bread in the kitchen. Fix yourself something to eat."

"I will."

She would have liked to see her daughter's face this morning, to have hugged her and to have drawn strength from the sight of her. The last thing Marisol wanted to do was to go out and beg for a job in a town she'd always hated—from people she'd always felt hated her. But for Toni, she would do it.

She went first to the courthouse. At one time, the county and the school district were the town's largest employers. She wasn't qualified to be a teacher, but surely she could handle work as a clerk in one of the county offices.

The woman behind the counter's eyes widened when she saw Marisol. "You're Lamar Dixon's wife," she said. "I mean widow."

"I'm Marisol Luna. I'd like to apply for a job."

The woman's eyes narrowed. "Doing what?"

"Anything." Marisol forced herself to meet the woman's critical gaze. "What openings do you have?"

The woman shook her head emphatically. "You couldn't work here."

"Why not?"

"You can't have a criminal record and work for the county government."

Marisol stiffened. "I don't have a criminal record," she said. "I was acquitted. That means I was found not guilty."

"I know what it means." The woman's lips were a thin, straight line in her stern face. "I don't think anyone would want to hire you. It wouldn't look good."

Marisol ground her teeth together, battling the urge to tell this woman exactly what she thought of her. "May I fill out an application?" she asked evenly.

"Fill it out all you want." The woman pulled a sheet of paper from a cubbyhole and sailed it across the counter, then turned away, muttering about people who "weren't any better than they should be."

Marisol fared little better at the other places she tried. The office supply owner asked why a woman "whose husband made all that money" would need to work.

Marisol chafed at explaining Lamar had gambled away most of his income, and she had spent the rest fighting for her life in court.

"Trust me, I need the job," she said instead. She didn't mention she only planned to stay in town a few months at the most; no sense giving anyone another reason not to hire her.

"Can't help you. I already got a high school girl who works part-time and that's all I need."

The librarian was more sympathetic. "I wish I could help you, I really do," she said. "But the county cut our budget this year and we had to let one of our librarians go. We're getting by with volunteers. But if you'd like to volunteer…"

The florist squinted at Marisol behind thick spectacles. "I know you," he said.

Who doesn't? she wanted to reply, but kept quiet and waited for him to say something about the trial. Instead, he startled her by saying, "You're Marisol Luna. I knew you in high school." His grin was more of a leer. "I remember when you jumped off the highway bridge. Stark naked." He chuckled. "That was really something."

She wanted to slap the grin right off his face, but, thinking of Toni, she repressed the impulse. "Do you have any job openings?" she asked.

He leaned across the counter toward her, his tone confiding. "I'd love to hire you, hon, but my wife would have a conniption if she thought the two of us were working together. So I'd better not. Though if you'd like to come back after I close up, maybe we could have a drink for old time's sake."

She moved on. Her feet hurt, and her mouth, neck and shoulders strained from holding her head high and smiling. Sweat pooled in the small of her back and she worried her antiperspirant had given up. She was also hungry and had a pounding headache. She tried to distract herself by looking at her surroundings. As she'd told Toni, the whole town looked better than it had when she'd left, with new awnings, fresh paint and flowers around the square. She recalled seeing an article in the travel section of the *Houston Chronicle* last year, which had touted Cedar Switch as a popular destination for weekend getaways, with a newly revitalized downtown, an abundance of bed-and-breakfast inns and restaurants and shops that catered to tourists.

The whole square now looked like something out of a Norman Rockwell painting— except for the hulking brown building two blocks west of the courthouse. Once a masterpiece of Victorian architecture, with elaborate wedding-cake trim, soaring columns and a stained-glass cupola, the Palace Hotel had been *the* social center of town when Marisol was a girl. Countless senior proms, wedding receptions and formal balls had been held in the upstairs ballroom.

Now the paint was faded and flaking, the windows broken or boarded up. Overgrown rose vines spilled across the front steps, bright pink petals scattered down the walk, as if left over from a long-ago wedding reception. A red-and-white metal For Sale sign was planted near the sidewalk.

Marisol stared at the once-grand building with a knot in her throat. When she looked back on her life in Cedar Switch, almost all of the good times were associated with the Palace Hotel. Seeing it so neglected and run-down made her doubt the reliability of her memories. Maybe her recollections of the past were as flawed as her judgment about Lamar.

She turned away, and hurried back to the square, mentally reviewing her employment options. She was running out of places to look for work. The bank, hardware store and Cherie's boutique had all turned her down, some more politely than others. Everyone had stared. Some had asked rude questions. No one had offered her a job, or any clue as to where she might find employment.

There was the grocery store out near the highway—though the thought of dragging dripping chickens and twelve packs of beer across the scanner made her recoil in revulsion. She stopped and studied the square for anything she might have missed. Her gaze rested on a white storefront in the middle of the block on the east side of the courthouse. The Bluebonnet Café.

There had been a café in that location when Marisol was a girl, though then it had been the Courthouse Café. Open for breakfast and lunch, it had done a good business, catering to downtown workers and shoppers and those who had dealings at the courthouse.

Restaurants almost always needed help, didn't they? And no special skills were needed for waitressing beyond a good memory, a certain grace and the ability to chat up the customers. Countless charity balls and cocktail parties had trained her well in those talents.

She squared her shoulders and walked to the corner to cross the street. With her luck, she didn't want to risk getting arrested for jaywalking. Even that would be enough to make her the top story in the evening news.

The café itself was a neat, white-painted room lined with red-leatherette booths, the center filled with small tables with blue-checked tablecloths and ladder-backed chairs.

"Can I help you?" an older woman with twin long gray braids, a white apron over overalls and T-shirt asked when Marisol stopped in the entrance.

"I'd like to apply for a job," Marisol said.

The woman gave her a curious look, and Marisol braced herself for comments about the trial, or Lamar, or even her infamous past in Cedar Switch. Instead, the woman said, "You're prettier than most we get in here. You ever wait-ressed before?"

Marisol shook her head. "But I'm very good with people."

"Can you carry a tray full of blue plate specials, that's the question."

"Yes, I can. I'm sure I can."

"All right." The woman opened a drawer and pulled out a single sheet of paper. "Fill that out."

Marisol completed the brief questionnaire, writing in the number and street of her mother's old house in the space for address. Even after twenty years, she could recall it easily. Staring at the address on the paper, she felt a sense of disorientation—the same feeling she'd had each morning in jail when she'd first awakened, as if at any minute she'd discover she'd only been dreaming. Lamar wasn't dead. She wasn't accused of killing him. Everything was all right again.

The woman returned, took the paper and glanced at it. "The pay is five dollars an hour plus tips," the woman said. "6:00 a.m. to 2:00 p.m. Can you start tomorrow?"

Marisol blinked. "You mean I'm hired?"

"If you want the job and you can do the work, yeah."

"Yes. I mean, thank you. I'll be here tomorrow." She'd meant to spend tomorrow getting Toni enrolled in school, but there would be time to do that in the afternoon. Toni would have to get herself up and onto the school bus each day, but the responsibility would be good for her.

"Thank you," Marisol said again, unable to keep back a smile. "Thank you." Then she hurried away, before the woman could change her mind. She had a job. A real job. She looked around, wishing she had someone she could tell. Some friend.

But the women she'd thought of as friends— other players' wives, women in her neighborhood and those with whom she'd served on the boards of various charities—had ceased to be friends the night Marisol was arrested. Not one of them had visited or written to her during her trial or in the long days leading up to it. She was no longer one of them.

That had been one more hurt, on top of losing her husband and learning the truth about all he'd done behind her back. One more thing to harden herself against. She straightened and walked toward her car. She'd celebrate tonight with Toni. As long as she had her daughter, she didn't need friends.

Scott pulled his car to the curb and studied the modest white brick house with a critical eye. This sort of place wasn't as attractive to buyers from Houston as the Victorians near the square, but given enough time he was sure he could find a buyer. He hoped Marisol wasn't disappointed in the price he thought he could get; to a woman used to living in a River Oaks mansion, the going rate for small-town residences probably seemed like pocket change.

He shut off the engine and glanced at his reflection in his rearview mirror, wondering why he was bothering. Marisol Luna wasn't going to be impressed by the likes of him. Besides, he had a girlfriend. Tiffany Ballieu, the blue-eyed blond sweetheart of his high school days, had sought him out last year, letting him know she was newly divorced and more than willing to pick up where they'd left off. Tiffany was sweet, respectable and exactly the sort of woman he needed in his life.

Carrying the folder with the comparables he'd pulled and a blank listing agreement, he made his way up the walk and rang the doorbell. He waited, and was about to ring a second time when the door creaked open a scant two inches and one bright brown eye studied him through the crack. "Hello?" said a soft female voice.

"I'm Scott Redmond," he said. "Here to see Marisol Luna."

"She doesn't want to talk to any reporters." The door started to close.

"I'm not a reporter," Scott said. "I'm a real estate agent. She talked to me yesterday about selling this house."

The door opened a little wider, and Scott saw half of a pretty, young face. "Mama went downtown to look for a job," the girl said. "I can't let you in."

A job? Did this mean Marisol planned to stay in Cedar Switch? Maybe she'd changed her mind about selling the house. "Do you think she'll be back soon?" he asked. "Could I wait out here for her?"

"I think she'll be back soon." The door opened wider still. The girl had a beautiful, oval face, long braids and long, thin arms and legs. "You can wait if you want."

"Thanks." He moved over to a green metal chair at one end of the porch.

The door closed, and he heard the rattle of a chain being moved. Then it opened again and the girl came out. "My name's Toni," she said, and leaned against the closed door, as if ready to retreat inside at any minute.

"Hi, Toni. What do you think of Cedar Switch?"

"Not much."

"Yeah. I guess it's not that impressive to someone from the city."

"Have you lived here a long time?"

"All my life." He glanced at her. She was taller and thinner than Marisol had been, but he could see her mother in her. "I knew your mother when she was about your age. We went to school together."

"Really?" She turned toward him, her expression eager. "What was she like then?"

How to explain the Marisol who had awed him so? "She was pretty, like you. And daring. She did things no one else would try."

"Really? What kind of things?"

He frowned. In addition to diving naked off the bridge, when assigned to write a paper on an important historical figure Marisol had reported on Sally Rand, the infamous fan dancer and stripper. Half the football team claimed to have slept with her, but Scott couldn't recall having seen Marisol in the company of any of them, so he suspected wishful thinking on their part. What was true was that she was frequently in trouble for mouthing off to teachers and was a familiar figure in detention hall her final year at Cedar Switch High School.

None of this was the sort of thing he could share with her daughter. "Your mother was very independent," he said. "The kind of person others looked up to and wanted to be like." At least, he'd felt that way.

"She never talks about growing up here," Toni said. "It's like it's some big secret or something."

"She probably doesn't want to bore you," Scott said. Everyone had secrets they didn't want to share, especially not with children.

He was saved from further comment by the arrival of the red Corvette. Marisol parked in the driveway and got out. Despite the heat, she looked fresh and vibrant, her hair pulled back in a ponytail, a tropical-print sleeveless dress bright against her tanned skin. "Scott," she said. "Have you been waiting long?"

"Not long." He held up the portfolio. "I came to discuss listing the house, if now's a good time."

"Now is fine. Come on in." She walked past them and led the way inside.

"Did you get a job?" Toni asked.

"I did." Marisol smiled. "I start tomorrow morning."

"Where will you be working?" Scott asked.

"I'm the newest waitress at the Bluebonnet Café."

She laughed at the obvious surprise on both their faces.

Scott had a difficult time imagining the elegant woman before him taking orders at the down-home restaurant. "Have you waited tables before?" he asked.

She shook her head. "No. But I told the woman there I could learn." She glanced at her daughter. "It'll be an adventure. And the hours will let me be here when you get home from school."

Toni rolled her eyes. "It's not like I need a babysitter," she said.

"I know." She patted Toni's shoulder. "Scott and I need to talk business for a bit, okay?"

"Okay." She headed down the hall and in a moment Scott heard a door close.

"She's a sweet girl," Scott said. "She reminds me of you at that age."

"I'm amazed you remember me. I'd better show you the house."

He was aware of being alone with her in rooms that still held the chill of long-unoccupied space. When her hand brushed his arm as she reached past him to flip a light switch, he felt a sharp stab of arousal. Her eyes met his and he sensed she felt it too. Then she turned away and the moment passed.

He forced himself to focus on the house. There wasn't much to see—three bedrooms, two bathrooms, formal dining and living rooms and the kitchen, where they ended the tour. "Everything seems to be in good repair," he said. "But that wood paneling in the dining room and the black and white tiles in the kitchen and bath scream 1970s. If you'd put some money into updating the place—paint over the paneling, and install new flooring and countertops, and maybe some new appliances—you'd get a much better price."

"I can't afford to remodel." She took two glasses from the kitchen cabinet. "I'm going to have some iced tea. Would you like some?"

"That would be good." He pulled out a chair and sat at the table, enjoying the view of her curvy backside and shapely legs as she pulled the pitcher from the fridge.

"I'm guessing my kitchen cabinets aren't what's making you smile that way," she said as she set the tea in front of him and joined him at the table.

Heat burned his cheeks. To cover his embarrassment at being caught ogling her, he opened the folder and shuffled through the papers. "I pulled the legal description at the courthouse, and some comparables of other sales of similar properties for you to look at. Judging by them, here's how much I think you can get for the place." He slid the listing agreement to her and pointed to the line for the selling price.

Her eyes scanned the paper, and she frowned. "I was hoping for a little more."

"We can ask, but the market is in a bit of a slump now, and these smaller places tend to sell more slowly. Again, if you'd remodel…"

She shook her head, and picked up a pen. "If this is the best we can do, then we'll do it." She signed with a flourish, then handed the papers back to him. "How long do you think it will take to find a buyer?"

"Tough to say. The average time on the market has stretched to five months, though of course I'll do my best to shorten that."

"Do what you can," she said. She looked around the kitchen. "It feels strange, being back here after so many years."

"There are some attractive new homes on the west side of town," he said. "Maybe after you've sold this place you could move to one of them."

"No, I'm not planning on staying. There's nothing for me here." Her eyes met his and he felt the impact of that gaze, and a leaden ache in his stomach. He could admit, if only to himself, that he hadn't completely set aside the fantasy of the two of them getting together. Having a relationship that went beyond agent and client. But her words made it clear she saw no possibility of that.

What did it matter, anyway, when she was so clearly out of his league? He'd trespassed in this world once before and proved he couldn't keep up. He changed the subject. "Who did you talk to at the Bluebonnet?"

"I didn't get her name. An older woman with braids. She was wearing overalls and an apron."

"That's Mary Sandifer, the owner. She and her husband bought the place from Marty Wakefield a couple of years ago. She's a good woman. The kind who doesn't suffer fools and isn't afraid to say what she means. She probably sensed you were a kindred spirit."

"Maybe I used to be that way." She traced a line of condensation down her glass. "I've learned to keep my mouth shut."

He studied her, at the fine lines at the corner of her eyes, the few strands of silver shining in her dark hair. She was still a beautiful woman, but there was an added depth to her now, a sense that she'd survived hard times and triumphed that only added to her attractiveness. "Has it been very hard for you?" he asked. "The trial, and everything that came out during it?"

"You mean that my husband was a lying, gambling cheat?" She smiled ruefully at his obvious shock. "I suspected there were other women all along, but I never dreamed he was so deep into debt—and with the mob, no less. It's a wonder he stayed alive as long as he did. But it was hard, yes. Hard to hear the accusations that were made about me, hard to lose my home. Hard to see Toni suffer."

"She seems to have come through it all right."

Marisol nodded. "As well as she could, I suppose." She took another long sip of tea, studying him over the rim of the glass. "Tell me about yourself. All I know is that you're Jay's son. I'm sorry I don't remember much from school."

"There's no reason you should. I was two years behind you." He replaced the papers in the portfolio, sorting through all the things he might tell her about himself. *I once had a huge crush on you,* or *I almost ruined my life a few months ago and am still trying to pull my reputation out of the cellar.* "There's nothing exciting to tell," he said. "I used to work for one of the big firms in town, but six months ago I opened a solo office in my dad's building. I've lived in Cedar Switch all my life. Guess I'm just a small-town kind of guy." While she was definitely not a small-town girl.

"Are you married?"

The question startled him. Was she merely making conversation, or was she truly interested? His heart beat faster at this idea. "I'm… seeing someone," he admitted, reluctantly.

"You probably think I'm being nosy," she said. "I don't mean it that way. It's just that I never thought *I'd* be single at this age and I wonder how it is for other people." She traced one finger around the rim of her glass, the gesture strangely sensual. Her nails were long, painted a pale pink. "I married Lamar when I was nineteen. We were together sixteen years. Now it's as if… I've not only lost my husband, I've lost my whole identity." She laughed, a jagged, desperate sound. "It's like being a teenager all over again, trying to find myself."

"I don't think there's any deadline on figuring out what you want to do with your life," Scott said. "At least I hope not. I'm not sure I've answered that question for myself yet."

She nodded, and pushed her glass away, then stood. "Thank you for stopping by. Is there anything else you need from me?"

"Not now." He gathered up his papers and prepared to leave, wishing he had an excuse to linger.

She walked him to the door, thanked him again, then shut the door behind him. Before he drove away, he glanced at the house once more, half hoping to catch a glimpse of her at a window.

But there was no sign of her. He checked the mirror, then pulled into the street. His newest client fascinated him, not so much for her notoriety, or even for the long-ago crush he'd had on her.

Marisol was independent and determined to keep her distance from everyone, and yet he sensed a deep longing for connection within her. That longing, more than anything, called to him. He shook his head, unsure how much of this perception was true, and how much was based on everything he'd believed about her when he was a boy.

He'd believed that she knew more about life than he could even guess.

That she'd been hurt, but didn't let it show.

That she was braver than anyone he knew.

And now? He still believed that she was brave and wise. With one smile, she'd reduced him to a stammering schoolboy. With one look, she'd reminded him what it meant to be a man. What it was like to want a woman not only for her looks, but for her mystery.

Chapter Three

Marisol reported for her first day of work at the Bluebonnet Café as jittery as someone who'd downed three cups of coffee, though she'd stuck to herbal tea at breakfast. She hadn't had a real job since a stint at McDonald's as a teenager, but she was determined to do her best.

Mary greeted her with a firm hello and handed her a black apron and an order pad. "We do things the old-fashioned way here," she explained as she led Marisol toward the kitchen. "Write the order down and give a copy to the cook." She introduced Marisol to the cook, Frank, and the other waitress, Paula.

"Just holler if you need help with anything,"

Paula, a diminutive blonde who wore bright pink lipstick, offered. "You'll get the hang of it in no time."

As it turned out, the worst part was not remembering which table ordered what, or even carrying the heavy trays without dropping them. The worst part was forcing herself to ignore the stares and whispers when diners realized who she was.

"What in the world are you doing working here?" a burly man with a luxuriant gray moustache asked as she refilled his coffee cup. "I thought I read Lamar Dixon had more money than God."

"Maybe he did," she said calmly. "But he pissed it all away."

That surprised a laugh from the man. Marisol turned and walked on shaking legs to replace the coffeepot on the burner.

"How's it going?" Paula asked, joining Marisol.

"Okay," Marisol said. Most people had been polite, and she'd pocketed fifteen dollars in tips in her first two hours. Not bad considering most people only wanted coffee and one of Mary's oversize cinnamon rolls.

"Business is up this morning," Mary said as she passed on her way into the kitchen. "I

reckon everyone wants to get a look at you."
She nodded to Marisol.

Marisol flushed. Paula patted her arm. "Don't
worry. The novelty will wear off in a few days
and you'll be as invisible as I am."

Paula left to take the order from a table of
truck drivers, who grinned and flirted. So much
for being invisible. Marisol took a deep breath
and went to clear the table the moustached man
had vacated. He'd left a five-dollar tip. She
stared at the bill, angry at the pity the gesture
implied, furious with herself for revealing the
desperateness of her situation to a stranger. Next
time someone had the nerve to ask what she was
doing here, she'd be glib, and tell them she was
rehearsing for a starring role in a movie about
a waitress—or thinking about writing a book.

She pocketed the bill with her other tips and
moved on to the next table, three women who
stared at her with open curiosity, but said not
a word.

By lunchtime, Marisol's feet and legs hurt
from standing so long, but she felt more comfortable taking orders and was congratulating
herself on mastering the knack of carrying a
loaded tray of food. On Paula's advice, she'd
made more of an effort to smile. Not only did it
improve her disposition, it had the added bonus

of unsettling those who gawked the most. They apparently hadn't expected an accused murderess to be so friendly.

A flutter of nerves struck her anew when Scott Redmond came into the café with his father. The sharp physical attraction she'd felt for him yesterday had caught her by surprise. After so many months of being forced to bury every emotion, such frank desire made her feel almost giddy with relief and wonder. That living, lusting, *female* part of her hadn't died along with Lamar. It had only been hiding, waiting for the right moment—or the right man?—to reappear.

The question remained as to what she would do about it. The thought of a solely physical affair, with no strings attached and no promises for the future, held all the appeal of forbidden fantasy. But she had Toni—and Scott himself—to consider. As much as she longed to be selfish for once, practicality and a cursed sense of responsibility interfered.

The two men sat at one of the booths assigned to her, and greeted her with warm smiles. "How's your first day going?" Jay asked.

"I think I'm getting the hang of it," Marisol said.

"She's doing great." Mary came up behind

her and put one hand on Marisol's shoulder. "I think I might let her stay."

"I'm glad to hear it," Scott said. His gaze met and held hers for a beat too long. Her heart thudded in her chest like a wild bird, proving she hadn't imagined the attraction between them.

He was the first to look away. He picked up the menu and studied it, then said, "I'll have a burger and a glass of iced tea."

"Give me the Reuben," Jay said. "And a Diet Coke."

She hurried from the booth to turn in their orders, aware of his gaze on her as she crossed the room. He'd watched her yesterday, too, checking her out as she fixed their tea. Clearly, he liked what he saw, just as she appreciated his broad shoulders and slim hips, the wiriness that was in direct contrast to Lamar's height and muscular bulk.

She collected chicken-fried steak dinners for a quartet of construction workers and started across the room, veering around a young man who'd inexplicably stopped in the middle of the room. She'd almost reached the table when a bright light blinded her, followed quickly by a second flash, and the unmistakable click of a camera shutter. A woman squealed. The young man who'd been stopped shoved a small tape recorder in front of her face. "Mrs. Dixon, what can you tell us about your new job here at the Bluebonnet Café?"

The tray slipped from Marisol's hands, chicken-fried steak, mashed potatoes and green beans flying. The camera flashed again and she ducked, shielding her face, while voices rose around her.

"Out! Out of here before I call the police!" Mary shouted at the reporter and photographer, who ignored her, continuing to take pictures and shout questions at Marisol.

Paula rushed over and began cleaning up the spilled food, while the construction workers complained loudly about Marisol's clumsiness and their ruined dinners. Mary continued to shout at the two intruders.

Panic and anger choking her, Marisol tore off the apron and flung it and her order pad onto the counter. She had to get out of here, lay low somewhere until things calmed down. She darted for the door, only to find her exit blocked by the reporter, who grinned and extended the microphone. "Is it true you're originally from Cedar Switch, Mrs. Dixon? What do the people here think of your notoriety?"

"I think if you don't move out of the way and stop blocking the door, I'll make you move."

Marisol hadn't thought of Scott as an imposing man before, but there was definite menace in his posture now as he glowered at the reporter.

"Better do as he says," Jay spoke from just behind his son.

The reporter glanced from one man to the other, then decided retreat was in order. With a sweeping bow, he indicated the door was clear.

Scott put one arm around Marisol and guided her down the sidewalk. "I didn't see your car in the lot or on the street. Did you walk?"

"I shouldn't leave," she said. "If there's somewhere I could hide for a few minutes…" She looked back toward the café as the photographer and the reporter exited.

"If you go back, so will they," Jay said. "We'll drive you home."

As they rounded the corner to the small parking lot behind the café, the camera flashed again. Scott lunged at the photographer, who laughed, then dove into a waiting car, which sped away.

"Sorry about that," Scott said as he helped Marisol into the backseat of a blue sedan, then climbed in after her. Jay took the driver's seat and drove slowly toward Marisol's house, circling the block a few times, looking for suspicious vehicles or persons, before pulling into her driveway.

"Maybe I should go back," Marisol said. She hated running away, like a coward. "I should have stood up to them."

"What would that have done but give them more pictures, and words they could misquote?" Scott asked. His face was flushed, his eyes dark with anger. Part of her wanted to throw her arms around him, to let him hold her and be the rescuer to her damsel in distress.

Except that she was through with men rescuing her. No man who was supposed to protect had ever done her any favors. And no good would come of letting Scott think she needed taking care of. "I'll be fine now," she said. She started to open the door and climb out of the car, but Scott's hand on her arm stopped her.

"Are you going to be okay?" he asked. "Do you want us to stay with you a while?"

"I'll be okay." She scanned the front yard and the street, but they were empty. "It doesn't look like they've found this place. At least not yet."

"Who were they?" Scott asked. "Do you know them?"

She shook her head. "They're probably from some gossip rag." She smoothed the front of her skirt. "I was hoping they wouldn't find me here in Cedar Switch."

"Was this what it was like for you in Houston?" Scott's face reflected his horror at the idea. "With people like that hounding you?"

"Pretty much. From the time I was released on bail until the trial ended and Toni and I left to come here there was always at least one group, sometimes more, parked in front of my house. They trailed me everywhere. We managed to avoid being followed here by leaving in the middle of the night and driving through back streets to lose the one car that tried to come after us."

"I'll call the police chief and ask him to keep an eye on your place," Jay said. "Chase away anybody who's loitering."

"Thank you, but you can't keep them out of public places," she said. "They know their legal rights." The horror of the scene in the café was beginning to set in—that first blinding flash, the flying tray of food. "Mary will never let me come back to work now," she said.

"I'll talk to her," Scott said. "It's not your fault—"

"No." She gripped his arm, silencing him.

"I don't need you to fight my battles for me. I'm not helpless."

He started to protest, then apparently thought better of it. "What will you do?"

"I don't know. I'll think of something." She opened the door and climbed out of the car. He didn't try to stop her this time, though she could feel his eyes on her as she unlocked the front door.

Inside, she locked the door and leaned back against it. What little peace she'd enjoyed since leaving Houston had been shattered. She could only imagine the headlines that would accompany the pictures those two lowlifes had taken: *Accused murderess reduced to slinging hash in small town café.* Or maybe *Billionaire's widow forced into menial labor.* The pictures and stories would make the rounds of all the Junior Leaguers who had once welcomed her as one of their own. They'd shake their heads and click their tongues and tell each other how they had always suspected Marisol was not really "their kind of people" and this only confirmed it.

Worse, how long would it be before those two men, or others like them, zeroed in on this house? How long would she and Toni have to barricade themselves inside before a more interesting scandal distracted her pursuers?

Toni. The thought of her daughter spurred her to action. She needed to telephone the school and ask them to have Toni wait in the office for her mother to collect her after school. Under no circumstances was she to go outside, and the school should be on the lookout for any suspicious characters hanging around the campus, especially anyone with a camera.

Toni would hate being singled out this way, especially on her first day. And she would, as usual, blame her suffering on her mother.

For her part, Marisol laid the blame firmly on Lamar, though fat lot of good that did, considering he was dead. What remaining love she'd had for the man upon his death had been leeched out of her by the ugly revelations of the trial and the suffering his mistakes and bad habits had brought on her and on Toni. The part of her heart that had once belonged to her handsome husband was now empty and cold. She wasn't sure she had the strength to risk ever trusting a man again.

Which made her reaction to Scott that much more suspect. Maybe her sudden desire for him fell into the same category as nervous laughter at funerals and the sensation of wanting to jump when standing on the balcony of a tall building—involuntary, misplaced emotions or misfiring synapses. In a way it was comforting to realize her body was still capable of feeling attracted to a man. And Scott was, after all, good-looking and charming.

But it would be a long time before her *mind* was ready to let a man into her life. And when it happened, it would be somewhere a long way from Cedar Switch, Texas. Her time here was merely an interlude while she regrouped, refreshed her finances and prepared herself for a new life, one far removed from either her glamorous days in Houston, or a childhood here in the sticks she'd spent twenty years working to forget.

Chapter Four

The ringing phone woke Scott the next morning at six thirty. "Have you seen the front page of today's *Houston Chronicle*?" a raspy voice demanded.

Scott sat up on the side of the bed and rubbed his eyes. "Marcus, is that you?" He checked the bedside clock. Apparently the real estate mogul was an early riser.

"Your picture is on the front page of the Houston paper, all cozied up to Lamar Dixon's infamous widow."

The words had the same effect as dunking his head in a bucket of ice water. "What?"

"I didn't know you knew Marisol Dixon,"

Marcus continued. He was a man who preferred asking questions to answering them.

"She's using the name Marisol Luna now," Scott said. "She's listed her house with me."

"I thought that River Oaks mansion was sold to pay her legal fees."

"She has a house here in Cedar Switch. She inherited it from her mother."

A crackling sound, like paper being rattled, reached his ears. "Since when do real estate agents cuddle up to clients in the backseat of cars?"

Marcus should have been a tabloid reporter. He made one innocent gesture sound so lurid. "She was ambushed by a reporter and a photographer in the Bluebonnet Café yesterday when my dad and I were there eating lunch," he said. "We helped her get away from them and gave her a ride home."

Help Marisol hadn't been particularly grateful for, he reminded himself.

"And now half the state thinks the two of you are involved." Even this early, Marcus sounded as if he'd been drinking straight bourbon and smoking cigars for hours.

"I don't care what they think," Scott said. Phone to his ear, he leaned over and grabbed a pair of jeans off the back of the chair he'd flung them across before crawling into bed last night and began to pull them on.

"Well, I care!" Marcus's shout startled Scott so much he almost dropped the phone.

"I'm not involved with Marisol," he said. Yes, there had been that moment when their eyes had locked in the café yesterday. In that briefest instant he'd felt the heat of desire and possibility arc between them once more.

A possibility that would go unfulfilled. Marisol was leaving town. And he was staying here, out of trouble.

"You'd better not be involved with her," Marcus growled.

Scott stiffened. "Even if I was, what difference would it make?" he said. "She was acquitted of the murder charges."

"Acquitted! All that means is she had good lawyers. It doesn't mean she was innocent."

Scott froze in the act of zipping the jeans, his hand tightening on the receiver. "Marisol did not murder her husband," he said, struggling to keep his voice even.

"And you know this how? Were you there?" Marcus's voice was a gravelly sneer.

"Of course I wasn't there." He finished zipping the jeans and began to pace. "I watched the trial and the prosecution clearly didn't have enough evidence to convict her. Besides, she had nothing to gain by her husband's death, and everything to lose. She *did* lose everything, which is why she moved back here and got a job waitressing in a café."

"Maybe she's just waiting for all the hubbub to die down, then she'll go away and spend the millions she's hiding from the government."

Scott took the receiver from his ear and stared at it. He was tempted to ask Marcus if he also believed in UFOs, alien abduction and other bizarre theories.

Marcus laughed again, a harsh, barking sound. "Don't you get it? It doesn't make a damn bit of difference what you think or even what the truth is. For the better part of a year, Marisol Dixon was the woman people loved to hate—the rich bitch socialite who offed her husband, the highest paid player in NBA history. Just because some jury said she didn't do it doesn't mean people believe it."

Scott knew a thing or two about being tried and found guilty in the court of public opinion, but Marcus's cynicism about Marisol annoyed him. "Thanks for letting me know about the picture in the paper," he said. "I'll lay low a few days and it will all blow over."

"And stay away from Marisol whatever-her-name-is."

"She's a client. If she wants to talk to me, I can't avoid her."

"Maybe you shouldn't have her as a client, then."

"What are you saying?"

"I'm saying that I hired you to represent my interests in this new development. The buyers I'm courting here are high rollers from Houston and Dallas—the kind of people who think the worst of a social climber like Mrs. Dixon. If they think you're associated with her, then that reflects badly on me."

The fact that Marcus had hired him to sell a bunch of golf course lots didn't give him the right to dictate who Scott could and could not associate with. He would have liked nothing better than to tell the man so, but that desire came up against hard reality. Those listings from Marcus were Scott's ticket back to both solvency and respectability. If he lost them, he may well lose his last chance to redeem himself.

"I took a big risk hiring you," Marcus reminded him. "Don't make me regret it." *Or you will regret it* was the unspoken codicil. Marcus had ruined people with better reputations than Scott who had gotten on his wrong side. He wielded the power that came with his wealth with all the subtlety of a war club.

"I promise not to do anything that would fuel any rumors about my association with Ms. Luna," Scott said stiffly. "Ours is strictly a business relationship." That was all that would ever be between them, but he would not—even at Marcus's insistence—refuse to do the one thing he could do for her, that is, sell her house.

"See that you don't. And keep Sunday open for me. I've got a group of investors coming down from Houston to look at the development. I think they'll be good for at least one lot each, maybe more."

"I'll be here," Scott said. "I'll let you go now. Goodbye." He hung up before Marcus could think of any more orders to give him. He sat on the side on the bed, heart thudding hard in his chest, the familiar feeling of wanting to escape almost overwhelming. Drugs had provided that kind of escape once, a floating euphoria that made all his problems disappear.

But he was stronger than that now. He could cope. He stood and went into the bathroom, where he chose a bottle from the medicine cabinet and shook out a single, small pill. He hated he'd traded one drug dependence for another, but a methamphetamine habit and the subsequent recovery had left him with a lingering anxiety disorder he kept under control with the help of a prescription and a meditation practice the Buddhist director of the treatment center where he'd spent three months had passed on him.

He finished dressing and made coffee and toast, then walked to the street and collected his copy of the Houston paper from the box at the end of the driveway. Sure enough, there on the lower right quadrant of the front page was a close-up of him and Marisol, his arm around her, their heads together, in the backseat of his father's car.

It was an intimate shot, her head tilted toward his, almost touching, her hair fallen forward to hide much of her face, only the curve of her cheek and lips and part of one eye showing. *Lamar Dixon's widow wastes no time finding new beau* read the caption beneath the photo.

They obviously hadn't talked to anyone in Cedar Switch about his relationship with Marisol, or they'd have learned pretty quickly he was her real estate agent, not her lover. Then again, he supposed men like those reporters never let truth get in the way of a good story.

He continued to stare at the photograph, at that moment frozen on the page. Marisol looked beautiful and vulnerable and he had never felt more protective. Had she seen this? What did she think? Should he call her and see how she was doing? Not out of any romantic interest, but because he wanted her to know she had at least one friend in this town.

He was still standing on his front porch, staring at the paper when the screech of tires drew his attention. He looked up as a familiar lime-green VW pulled to the curb.

The driver's side door opened and a lithe blonde dressed in navy trousers and a navy and white blouse stepped out.

"Tiffany? What are you doing here so early in the morning?" he asked. Tiffany Ballieu taught fourth grade at Cedar Switch Elementary school. Normally at this hour she'd be on her way to playground duty or bus duty or preparing her classroom for the day's lessons.

In the year they'd been dating, Scott had come to know her routines, and adopted the same predictable rhythm for his life: dinner together Wednesday and Friday nights, usually followed by sex. Nothing too wild, but satisfying and comfortable. Everything about Tiffany was satisfying and comfortable; she was never a source of anxiety or stress. She accepted and loved him with no special effort on his part, and he appreciated this as well as all her other good qualities.

Instead of answering his greeting this morning, however, she leaned back into the car and retrieved something from the front seat. As she walked toward him, Scott saw it was a folded newspaper. His breakfast felt like mud in his stomach.

"What is the meaning of this?" She thrust the paper at him.

"It doesn't mean anything," he said, not bothering to look at the photo.

"Lamar Dixon's widow wastes no time finding new beau," she read. "How is that nothing?"

"My father and I were eating lunch in the café when that photographer and a reporter showed up," he said. "We helped her get out of there, that's all."

"So she's just some stranger you helped out of the goodness of your heart." She stared at the photo again. "You look awfully cozy for strangers."

"Marisol isn't exactly a stranger. We knew each other in school, and she's listed her house here with me."

"Neither of those are any reason for you to

be snuggling up with her in the backseat of a car."

He crossed his arms and frowned at her. He'd always thought of Tiffany as easygoing and reasonable. Her jealousy over something so innocent annoyed him. "We're not *snuggling*, Tif. The photographer framed the shot for the effect he wanted. These guys are out to make money, not tell the truth."

"It's humiliating," she said. "Everyone knows you and I are dating, and now they'll see this and they'll think you left me for some rich, glamorous...*floozy*."

The old-fashioned word almost made him laugh. Except that he was still too annoyed at Tiffany's reaction—or rather, *over*reaction. "Marisol isn't rich," he said. "And she's not a floozy."

"But you obviously think she's glamorous." She pressed her lips together in a pout.

When he didn't respond, she launched into a fresh assault. "What is she doing here, anyway?" she said. "Cedar Switch doesn't have a Social Register for her to crash, or fancy parties and country clubs where she can show off her designer dresses and shoes."

Since when was Tiffany opposed to parties, or fancy dresses or shoes? Did she really feel threatened in some way by Marisol's arrival in town? "She came here to avoid publicity and start over," he said. "She's a widow with a teenage daughter and this is her hometown, after all."

Tiffany wrinkled her nose. "I hear she's driving around in a red Corvette," she said. "And she wasn't even here two days before her picture was in the paper. Those aren't the actions of someone who truly wishes to lay low."

"The photographer wasn't her fault. He must have followed her here."

Tiffany's eyes narrowed to catlike slits. "You certainly know a lot about your *client*."

He was tired of defending himself and Marisol against these accusations. "Marisol is a friend," he said firmly. "She needs friends right now. I'm not going to apologize for that."

"What if I asked you not to see her again? For my sake."

He stared at her, unsure if she was serious. She looked determined, which only made him angry. "You don't have a right to dictate my friendships."

"I'm the woman you love. That ought to give me some rights."

Silence stretched between them, painful and heavy. He knew she was waiting for him to reassure her that he did love her, and that she was the only woman for him. He opened his mouth, but couldn't bring himself to say the words.

He liked Tiffany. He enjoyed being with her. She was intelligent, fun and a good lover. Lately, she'd been hinting strongly that she wanted to get married, and he'd almost talked himself into buying a ring and giving it to her for her birthday next month. After all, it was time he settled down, and he couldn't imagine anyone with whom he felt more settled than Tiffany.

Then Marisol had come to town, and he'd been reminded of other dreams he'd once had for his life—of exciting adventures and great passions. He knew intellectually that all those things would be a mistake. He hadn't the temperament for them now, if he ever had. Hell, he couldn't get through the day without medication—what was getting involved with a woman like Marisol going to do to his ability to cope?

No, the smart thing to do was to keep his life on an even keel, to work on building his real estate practice and restoring his reputation.

Yet sliding into an easy life with Tiffany, into a marriage built on friendship and comfort rather than soul-gripping love, now felt like surrendering. Giving up.

The hardness went out of her face as she watched him, replaced by disappointment and sorrow. "I guess this means we're through," she said, and burst into tears.

He didn't go to her, merely stood rooted to the floor of the porch as she whirled and raced to her car.

It wasn't that he was in love with Marisol—he hardly knew her. But her sudden return to his life had awakened him out of the safe and comfortable stupor he'd fallen into since emerging from rehab almost a year ago. He'd been so fearful of slipping into old dangerous habits he hadn't allowed himself to do anything that would call forth strong feelings of any kind.

Yet less than forty-eight hours after meeting Marisol again he'd been enraged on her behalf, risked public censure defending her, stood up—in a small way—to Marcus, and steeled himself against Tiffany's tears. He felt stronger than he had in months, yet aware that he was dancing on the edge of a chasm. He'd fallen in once before, and narrowly escaped with his life.

He didn't know how much further he dared

to go, but he wanted to find out. Marisol had reminded him of what it meant to be alive again. Opening himself up to that kind of life—to both the joys and pain that were part of it—was a scary prospect, but one he welcomed after months of numbness. He couldn't retreat now. He could only go forward into whatever good—or bad—the future had in store for him.

Mary came to see Marisol the afternoon after the picture ran in the paper. "I brought you your pay for the hours you worked, and the tips that were in your apron," she said, handing over an envelope fat with cash.

Marisol ushered her inside, searching over her shoulder for any sign of the photographer's return. So far neither he nor the reporter had tracked her to this house, or bothered Toni at school, but she remained wary. Any hope she'd had of real privacy in this out-of-the-way town had been pure fantasy. The public's continued fascination with her and her tragedy amazed her. Lamar was dead, the trial was over—couldn't they move on to something else?

"I'm sorry about what happened yesterday," she said, when she joined Mary on the living room sofa. "I shouldn't have dropped the tray and run out of there that way, but I panicked."

She'd done the weak thing and allowed Scott and his father to talk her into leaving.

"It's okay." Mary smoothed her hands down the front of her khaki slacks. She was a thin woman, with knobby fingers and wrists, fine hair curling around her face like a child's. "We cleaned it up and everything calmed down after you left." She cleared her throat and raised her head to meet Marisol's eyes. "You'll understand if I don't ask you to come back?"

Marisol nodded, the ache in the pit of her stomach growing. Part of her had known this was coming, though she'd hoped not.

"You did a good job, especially for a first day," Mary said. "But it's too disruptive to my business, and not fair to the other employees, and the customers, to have people in there just for the sake of…of gawking."

"I know." Marisol swallowed hard, and straightened her back. "I'll find something else. Something that isn't so public." Maybe she could get a job clerking at the courthouse, or doing secretarial work in an office somewhere.

"I'm glad you understand." Mary stood abruptly, clearly anxious to leave. "Good luck."

Right. As if Marisol believed in luck anymore. She saw Mary to the door, then locked it behind her. As much as she wanted to stay hiding in here for the next few weeks or months until the house sold and she was able to move, the balance in her bank account was too small to comfortably rely on for an undetermined amount of time. Besides, hiding felt like letting the creeps win. She had no reason to be ashamed of showing her face in town.

She'd been standing up to adverse publicity for months; no reason to stop now.

The next morning, wearing dark sunglasses, her hair concealed by a brightly patterned silk scarf, she dropped Toni at school and set out once more to look for work. Having hit all the obvious places during her first job hunt, she was forced to dig deeper. She stopped at dentists' offices, small law firms and even the pool hall, where the owner blew out a cloud of cigarette smoke and told her they had all the help they needed, but she was welcome to a drink "on the house" if she wanted to tell him what *really* happened to her husband.

She trudged down the sidewalk, every step reminding her of all the reasons she'd been so anxious to leave this town in the first place. Though new businesses and people had moved here in her absence, it was still a small, insular place where it was difficult for newcomers, or anyone different to break in.

She passed the shuttered Palace Hotel and paused to stare at its derelict beauty. The For Sale sign was faded and rusting. It had obviously been there for a long while. For the first time, she noticed a second, red and black sign posted to the right of the front entrance. *Property of MH Investments. Trespassers will be prosecuted.*

MH Investments. Did that mean someone had bought the hotel with intentions to refurbish it? It would take a lot of work—and money—to restore the building to its former glory, but she thought it would be worth doing. There couldn't be very many examples of Victorian-influenced Gothic Revival architecture left in this part of the state.

Her gaze shifted to the top floor of the building, where rusty iron grating covered the tall windows. Mrs. Peabody's Dance Academy had held a recital in that upper ballroom every spring. Marisol could still smell the chalk-and-dance wax aroma peculiar to those events. Her last recital, when she'd been fifteen, she'd danced a solo choreographed for her by Mrs. Peabody herself, who proclaimed Marisol one of her most talented students.

Staring at the hotel now, with its fading paint and boarded-up windows, Marisol felt anger mixed with sadness. She'd lost so much—her mother, her husband and her reputation. She hated to see her memories destroyed as well.

On impulse, she crossed the street and hurried down one block to the courthouse. The clerk greeted her with open curiosity. "I heard what happened at the Bluebonnet yesterday," she said. "Doug Mayfield said chicken-fried steak and mashed potatoes were everywhere."

Marisol flushed. "When that flash went off in my face, I was so startled I dropped the tray."

"How in the world did those reporters find you here, anyway?" the clerk asked.

Marisol shook her head. "I don't know. I wish they hadn't."

"I guess you can find out just about anything about anybody these days, huh?" the clerk said. "I mean, with the internet and all."

"I guess so." Marisol looked around at the scuffed counters and green-painted walls, which hadn't changed since her girlhood. "I was hoping you could give me some information."

"That depends. What you need?"

"Who is MH Investments? And what do they plan to do with the old Palace Hotel?"

"That's Marcus Henry. You haven't heard of him?"

Marisol shook her head.

"Stay around here long and you will. He's only the richest man in the county. Some people say he pretty much saved the town, developing new resort neighborhoods that bring in wealthy folks from the cities, and advertising Cedar Switch as a great place to visit. We've got all kinds of businesses catering to tourists and weekend residents now. And his newest development, a golf course community out near Lake Meredith is supposed to be the biggest yet."

"Sounds like quite a guy," she said dryly. She'd met movers and shakers like him before— men with a knack for spotting a bargain and turning it into a healthy profit. They made their headlong dash for wealth easier for the locals to swallow by selling it as pure altruism. They may have been lining their pockets, but they were also "building up the community" and "promoting the town." Still, Marcus Henry probably had the kind of money needed to restore the hotel.

"What does he plan to do with the Palace Hotel?" she asked.

"Last I heard, he's going to tear it down and put in loft apartments. He's just waiting for the permits from the Commissioner's Court.

Though considering what an eyesore the old hotel has become, I don't imagine he'll have any problem getting what he needs." She made a snorting sound. "Not that Mr. Henry and his money ever have much trouble in that department."

Marisol nodded, feeling deflated. Loft apartments. Was there really anybody in Cedar Switch who *wanted* a loft apartment? Marcus Henry would probably convince them they did.

"Anything else you need?" the clerk asked.

"No. Wait, yes. Do you know whatever happened to Mrs. Peabody? She taught dance here for years."

"Everybody knew Mrs. Peabody," the clerk said. "My girls took classes from her right up until she died this winter."

"She's dead? But she wasn't that old," Marisol protested.

The clerk nodded. "She was sixty-four, though she looked ten years younger, and was more flexible than I'll ever be. They said she had a brain aneurysm. She was walking across the parking lot at the Piggly Wiggly with a bag of groceries in each hand and she just fell over. Dead before anyone could even get to her."

"What happened to her students?"

"The dance school closed. Some people

drove to Beeville for lessons, but it's over an hour away, so most people just quit." She shook her head. "I know my girls really miss it."

The phone rang, and the clerk left to answer it. Marisol turned and walked back outside. Mrs. Peabody dead. She could hardly believe it. Her classes had been the high point of Marisol's life in Cedar Switch. Often over the years she'd thought of contacting her teacher again and telling her how much dancing had meant to Marisol, but she never had.

The hotel was going to be torn down and Mrs. Peabody was gone—it was as if all the things she'd once loved were being taken from her, a little at a time.

She gave herself a mental shake. Forget the past. She had to focus on the future. Scott had said it might take months to sell her house, and even one emergency could wipe out her bank account before then. She had to find a way to bring in extra money, but a notorious socialite with no in-demand job skills obviously wasn't considered an ideal hire by employers in Cedar Switch.

Think, she silently demanded. *What can you do?*

She had experience entertaining—could she be a caterer? She made a face. She was a competent, but not a creative cook. And a catering business probably required a lot of special equipment and even licensing.

She had plenty of experience shopping, but she doubted if most people in Cedar Switch had need of a personal shopper.

She'd served on a lot of charity boards and committees, but she couldn't think of a way to translate that into a paying job.

She passed the hotel on the way to her car, and turned her head to avoid the sad sight. She thought once more of Mrs. Peabody. Her passing had left a real hole in the community, not only in the loss of her personally, but the loss of the school that had trained generations of young girls and boys in tap, ballet and modern dance.

That was it! Inspiration stopped Marisol on the sidewalk, and the first real happiness she'd felt in months made her giddy. She could teach dance. She'd kept up with classes over the years, and it wouldn't take a lot of fancy equipment. She'd clear out the front room and hang mirrors on the walls, and mount dance bars. She'd be home with Toni.

Getting students shouldn't be too hard. She'd advertise in the paper. Maybe she could even find out the names of Mrs. Peabody's former students and contact them.

She raced to her car, head full of plans, eager to share her good news with someone. But who? Toni wouldn't be home from school for hours and she was close to no one in town.

Then she thought of Scott. She should probably consult him about the changes she wanted to make to the house to transform it into a dance studio, and make sure they wouldn't affect the value of the building or interfere with a sale. Besides, he and his father were the closest thing she had to friends in this town.

When he'd put his arm around her and led her from the café yesterday, she'd allowed herself the luxury of leaning on him for a few minutes, drawing on his strength, his solid presence the first real protection she'd felt from the censure of others in a long time.

Thankfully, that moment of weakness had passed. She was the only person who could be depended upon to look after herself and Toni. It would be good to let Scott see that she was doing all right now. She had a plan for her future and didn't need him or any other man to take care of her.

But that resolve still didn't prevent her from wanting to share her idea with him.

Chapter Five

Marisol burst into Scott's office in a whirl of bright silk and floral perfume. The dejected woman of yesterday had been replaced by this radiant, smiling beauty. He rose to greet her, returning the smile, his own spirits soaring at the sight of her in spite of his determination to resist his attraction to her. "What a nice surprise," he said. "You're looking much better today."

"I'm feeling better." She dropped into the chair in front of his desk and grinned at him. "I've decided to open a dance studio at my house. What do you think?"

"A dance studio?" He blinked. "What brought this on?"

"It's perfect, don't you see?" She leaned toward him, eyes shining. "I can earn money without having to rely on someone else for a job. Since Mrs. Peabody passed away, her former students have been having to drive to Beeville for lessons—or they've given them up altogether. I have lots of experience, so I know I could teach."

Her ability to seize on a creative idea and act on it so quickly impressed him. Not that many months ago, *he'd* had a reputation as a quick-thinking go-getter. But since returning from rehab he'd felt mired in sand, deliberating too long over even minor decisions. Marisol's enthusiasm was bracing, and contagious. "It sounds perfect," he said.

"I'll need to make a few changes to the house—clear the furniture from the living room and put up some mirrors and dance bars. That won't affect the value, will it?"

"Not as long as the new owners can easily remove anything you add."

"I won't do anything they can't undo." She sat back, lips pursed in thought. "This won't make it more difficult to sell, will it?"

"It might deter some buyers," he admitted. "The market is very tight right now. But

I wouldn't let that stop you if this is what you really want to do."

"After being turned down by everybody and her sister in my search for a job, I don't see that I have any choice. Besides, this is what I really want to do. I love dancing." She took a deep breath and straightened her shoulders, which thrust her breasts forward, making him momentarily lose his train of thought.

He forced his eyes away and cleared his throat. "I can give you the name of a good contractor, to help you with installation of the mirrors and other things," he said.

"That would be great. I'd like to do some painting, too, to freshen things up."

He opened a side desk drawer and took out a business card from the stack he kept there and handed it to her. "Damon Wright is a great guy. He's done everything from major remodels to minor repairs for my clients and they've always been happy with his work."

"Thanks." She tucked the card into her purse. "Maybe you can give me some other information I need, too."

"Sure. Whatever you need."

"I need to find out how to get in touch with a man named Marcus Henry."

He couldn't have been more startled if she'd

asked him to recommend a bookie. "Why do you want to get in touch with him?" he asked.

"I understand he's the MH in MH Investments—the company that owns the old Palace Hotel?"

Scott nodded. "That's right. He owns a lot of property around town."

"Do you know him? What's he like?"

"I know him." As for her second question, how could he describe Marcus Henry? The man was smart, rich, and used to getting his own way. Some women thought him handsome, though Tiffany had described him as hard. "He's a shrewd businessman," Scott said finally.

Marisol nodded. "So if I'm going to ask him to do something to benefit the community, I need to make sure he sees the benefit to himself and his business."

"What are you up to?" Scott asked. "What do you want Marcus to do that will supposedly benefit the community?"

"I want him to give up his plan to tear down the old hotel and build condos. I want him to help restore the old building for use as offices and maybe a community center. Don't you think Cedar Switch could use something like that?"

Scott stared at her, amazed at the audaciousness of the idea, as well as the complete impracticality. "It would take hundreds of thousands of dollars to restore the old hotel," he said. "It's a fire trap and I'm sure none of the electrical or plumbing is up to code."

"It's a beautiful old building of historical significance to this town," she said. "As for the expense, there are grants to help with that sort of thing." She waved her hand as if they were discussing small change. "I've served on a lot of committees that tackled restorations and conversions like this. It seems like a big job, but the end result is more than worth the effort."

Scott shook his head. "I can give you Marcus's number, but don't expect him to listen to you. Once he's made up his mind to do something he doesn't change it."

She gave him an arch look. "Maybe I can change his mind."

Scott scribbled Marcus's number onto a sticky note, his stomach in knots. Maybe Marisol *would* persuade Marcus to change his mind. Marcus had a reputation with women. Every time Scott had seen him, he'd sported a different young beauty on his arm. Maybe the developer would take one look at Marisol's lustrous hair, shining eyes and feminine curves and decide he wanted her more than he wanted the old hotel. And Marisol might return his affections.

After all, she'd been married to a rich, power-ful man for sixteen years, so that was obviously the type she preferred.

He slid the paper toward her, but held it down when she tried to take it. "Just some friendly ad-vice," he said, looking into her eyes. "Marcus looks after Marcus, so don't trust him too much."

Sadness filled her eyes. "I've learned the hard way not to trust anyone," she said. She tugged the paper from beneath his fingers and slipped it into her purse. "I'd better go now. I shouldn't keep you."

"It's all right. I was going to call you this af-ternoon to see how you were doing."

She hesitated, then sat back in the chair. "I'm better now that I have a plan," she said. "Mary came by this morning and paid me for my one and only day at the café."

"How's Toni?" he asked.

Marisol rolled her eyes. "Toni is a teenager, what can I say? She hates school. She hates me for dragging her away from all her friends and bringing her to this place." She looked away, out the front window toward the street. From here, Scott had a view of the Baptist church and a discount store. "I can't say I blame her for that."

"You must not hate this town too much," he said, "if you want to save the old hotel."

"I hate to see beautiful things destroyed."

The passion in her voice caught him off guard. But then, everything about this woman unsettled him. "How did you find out about the hotel?" he asked.

"I saw the sign when I was out job-hunting this morning and I asked at the courthouse."

"No luck with the jobs, huh?"

She shook her head. "That's one reason teaching dance is so perfect. Nobody wants an employee who's going to draw so much negative attention."

"The picture in the paper today probably didn't help," he said.

She sat up straighter. "What picture?"

"You haven't seen today's *Chronicle*?"

She shook her head. "I quit reading newspapers after Lamar was killed. I got sick of reading all the nasty rumors about me and our marriage."

"Never mind, then. I shouldn't have said anything."

"You've let the cat out of the bag now. Do you have a copy of the paper? I'd like to see."

Reluctantly, he slid the folded paper from a pile on the corner of his desk and opened it to the picture of the two of them in the back of the car. She studied it for a moment, then to his surprise, she smiled. "I've seen worse," she said. "Don't you love how they managed to make the two of us seem so cozy? I guess any scandal sells better with a hint of sex."

"I guess so," he said, the words emerging in a croak. Would she be so amused if she knew how often his own thoughts of her and sex had converged?

"I hope this didn't cause you any trouble," she said, tapping the picture. "I don't guess your girlfriend was too happy about it."

"She wasn't," he said. He cleared his throat. "Not that it matters. She and I have split up."

Marisol's eyes widened. "Not over this, I hope."

"She was upset about the picture, but there was more to it than that. She wanted to get married, but I wasn't ready for that."

"Don't tell me you're one of those men who hates the thought of commitment. As if you're going to be a boy forever."

Is that how she saw him—as a boy? "I don't have anything against marriage," he said stiffly. "I just didn't think Tiffany was the woman I wanted to spend the rest of my life with."

"I can't say I'm eager to have a ring on my finger again anytime soon," she said. "But I don't necessarily want to be a nun, either."

This provocative statement was delivered with a flirtatious smile that sent a jolt of heat straight to his groin. "No, I can't see you as a nun" he heard himself say.

"I don't imagine a man like you will remain unattached too long," she said. Her voice was soft. Seductive.

"Not if the right woman comes along." So much for staying away from danger. She'd pulled him in up to his hips.

They looked at each other for a long moment, heat shimmering between them. At one gesture from her, he would have come around the desk and pulled her into his arms. But he held himself back, waiting for her.

"We should talk more about this." Eyes still locked to his, she rose slowly. "I should be going now. Toni will be home soon."

Talk was the last thing he wanted to do with her, but he willed himself to appear calm and unaffected. He walked her to the door, and watched her drive away, the red Corvette standing out among the pickup trucks and sedans parking along the street. Like the car she drove, Marisol didn't belong here.

She probably didn't belong in his life, either, but she was here now, and he wasn't strong enough to deny himself whatever she offered.

He returned to his desk and tried to focus on the online listing for a new property he was handling, but his thoughts kept returning to Marisol and the conversation they'd had. No telling how Marcus would react when she hit him with her proposal for restoring the old hotel. The developer had his mind fixed on building those lofts. He'd even mentioned having Scott handle the listing for them if the golf course sales went well.

Considering Marcus's response to Scott's picture in the paper with Marisol this morning, Scott would be better off if he turned the listing for Marisol's house over to another agent. If she stirred up sentiment against Marcus's plans to raze the hotel, it would only mean more trouble Scott didn't need.

He closed down the computer file and swiveled his chair to face the door once more. He wished he could tell Marcus Henry to take his business and shove it. But if Scott did that, he might as well pack his bags and leave town, what little reputation he had left in tatters.

It wouldn't matter so much to him. But it would break his father's heart. His dad had poured everything he had into saving Scott from himself. A man didn't repay that kind of debt by walking away from everything his father had given him.

But he wouldn't let Marcus bully him, either. Scott would do a good job for Marcus, and he'd do a good job for Marisol as well. Scott's pride demanded he see this deal through with Marcus.

But his heart compelled him to help a friend in need. No matter where the sexual attraction between them led, he was convinced Marisol needed his friendship too, whether she'd admit it or not. He was determined to stand by her, no matter what grief Marcus gave him. Doing so might not improve his reputation, but it would go a long way toward rebuilding the faith in himself he'd come close to throwing away.

Marisol began clearing out the living room as soon as she arrived home. Moving the heavy furniture into the spare bedroom and den left her breathless and sore, but she welcomed the opportunity to burn off some of the nervous energy that had been building ever since she'd walked into Scott's office.

Nervous energy—ha! Nothing short of plain, old-fashioned lust had taken hold of her. Maybe her elation over her plan to teach dance and her excitement over doing something positive to improve her and Toni's future had burned away the last of the black fog that had shrouded her for the past year. Once the cloud had parted, there was Scott. Handsome, compassionate, sexy Scott. And her body had reminded her brain in no uncertain terms that she was a woman who had been without a man for far too long.

So what was she going to do about it? She shoved against the heavy sofa, moving it a few inches closer to the hallway. In the aftermath of Lamar's death and during the months leading up to and including her trial, she'd been too focused on proving her innocence and protecting Toni to think about anything else. Now, sex—specifically, sex with Scott—was on her mind constantly.

The loneliness had started long before then, of course. In the last year of their marriage, she and Lamar had led largely separate lives. She'd been involved in charity work and raising Toni, while he'd partied hard with new friends who made her increasingly uncomfortable. "Friends" who would eventually be the cause of his death, though no one had been able to prove that.

That was all behind her now. She was starting over, with a different kind of life. This stopover in Cedar Switch was a necessary interruption, but who was to say she shouldn't make the most of her stay here? Why not enjoy a discreet fling with a handsome guy? A no-strings-attached affair to prove to herself she was still a desirable woman.

"Mom, what are you doing?"

Marisol started, guilt as unwelcome as a rash washing over her at the sound of her daughter's voice. Not that Toni could read Marisol's mind, but still...

Toni stood in the front door, staring at the almost-empty room. "Why are you moving the furniture?" she asked.

"I'm going to open a dance studio here at the house." Marisol straightened and tucked a stray lock of hair behind her ear. "I'm going to put in mirrors and dance bars, and some new paint. What do you think?"

"What made you decide this?"

"The woman who ran the dance studio here died earlier this year and her students were left without anywhere close by to study." Marisol shoved the sofa another few inches. "This will be perfect. It'll bring in the money we need and I'll always be right here if you need me."

"You're going to have people coming *here*? To the *house*?" Toni dropped her backpack beside the door and looked at Marisol as if she suspected her mother had lost her mind.

"Yes. That will keep my costs down and allow me to have a flexible schedule."

Toni's expression was no less horrified. "So the people I go to school with could be coming here, to this dinky house, and see you dressed in a leotard?"

"Most of your classmates live in houses pretty much like this one," Marisol said. "And I'll have you know I still look good in a leotard." She smiled, letting Toni know she was teasing, but the girl wasn't going to be placated.

"You never would have done something like this if we were still living in River Oaks," she said.

Marisol's smile vanished. "We're not in River Oaks now. Things are different." She looked around the disorganized room, the old-fashioned furniture all pushed to one corner, the floor dusty, the windows in need of cleaning. She'd have her work cut out to make this into a studio. But she'd welcome the distraction of physical labor. "Scott says it shouldn't hurt the value much to put in the dance bars and mirrors," she said, thinking out loud. "I can take them down when the place sells."

"You already talked to him about this? Before you talked to *me*?"

Marisol winced at the hurt in Toni's voice.

"I wanted to make sure it was okay to install the mirrors and things before I made a definite decision," she said.

"You should have hired a woman to sell your house."

Marisol studied Toni, who stared at the floor, bottom lip jutting out in a pout. Since when did Toni care about Marisol's choice of real estate agent? "Scott was recommended by a friend," she said. "I don't see what difference it makes if he's a man."

"A man who keeps *staring* at you," Toni said.

"Staring? Toni, what are you talking about?"

"I can't believe everything in my life is going to hell," she said, and bolted from the room.

Marisol went after her. Toni had shut her out too often these days. She eased open the bedroom door and looked at her daughter, who sat on the side of the bed, shoulders slumped, unsuccessfully trying to hold back tears.

"Tell me what's really wrong," Marisol said. She plucked a couple of tissues from a box beside the bed and handed them to Toni, then sat beside her, close but not touching. "Are things not going well at school?"

"They all hate me!" Toni blew her nose.

"They think I'm a snob because I don't dress the way they do. They call me rich bitch."

Anguish mixed with rage made a hard knot in Marisol's chest. How could anyone not love her beautiful little girl? She wanted to march down to the school and tell every one of those students—and their parents—exactly what she thought of them. But she settled for gently stroking Toni's hair. "It sounds to me as if they're jealous," she said. "But I know that doesn't make it any easier."

"Was it like this when you went to school here?" Toni asked.

Marisol hesitated, debating how much she should tell her daughter. "I'm sure no one was jealous of me," she said. "But I think at any school it's tough to be different."

Toni looked at her with a mix of curiosity and teenage skepticism. "How were you different?"

"For one thing, until my mother remarried, I was poor. And there weren't a lot of minorities here then." And in Cedar Switch, if not in all schools, once a student was saddled with a certain label, it was difficult to change others' perceptions. "I know it's hard for you," she said. "You were always so popular at your other school."

Toni looked at her mother with tear-filled eyes. "Why can't we go back there?" she asked. "Why can't I go back home to my friends?"

"I wish we could do that," Marisol said. "But you know the house was sold to pay my lawyers and your father's debts. I don't have the money left to buy another in that school district. And you know how we couldn't make a move there without the media hounding us. We couldn't go on living that way."

"Some kids were talking today about your picture in the paper this morning—with some guy's arm around you." Toni's voice shook, and she blew her nose again.

Marisol rested her hand on her daughter's back, wishing she knew the right words to say, to offer some real comfort. "That was Scott," she said. "He and his father were at the café when the reporters came in and they helped me get away. That's all there was to it, no matter what the paper tried to make it look like." Not that she wasn't toying with the idea of there being more than casual friendship between her and Scott. That part didn't concern Toni. If and when Marisol took up a physical relationship with a man, she'd make certain Toni never knew about it.

Toni sniffed. "You wouldn't want to date

anyone now that Dad's gone, would you?" she asked.

Marisol hesitated. She'd promised herself she would never lie to Toni, but how could she explain a woman's needs to a girl? "I'm not interested in dating anyone right now," she said. "I want to work and take care of you, then find a good place for the two of us to start over. A better place."

Toni chewed her bottom lip. "I wish Daddy hadn't died," she whispered.

Marisol put her arm around the girl, and Toni laid her head on her shoulder. "I know," she said soothingly. "It was a horrible thing for all of us." As much as Lamar had hurt her, if she had the choice to go back and pick up their marriage where they had left off, without him dying, she would do so. She would make that sacrifice to restore to Toni the privileged life she'd always known.

"Who killed him?" Toni asked. "Do you think the police will ever find out?"

The question startled Marisol. In all these months, it was one Toni had never asked. Marisol struggled to find the right answer, one that would reassure and comfort her. "I don't know." She hesitated, then said, "He was hanging out with some not-very-nice people. I think he got into trouble he couldn't get out of."

Toni raised her head and looked at her mother. "The paper said he owed gambling debts to organized crime," she said. "That's like the mob, right?"

"Where did you read that?" Marisol had worked hard to keep all the sordid details about her father from Toni.

"My friend Kasey brought the papers to school. I asked her to." Toni raised her chin, defiant. "I'm not a little kid. I had a right to know what was going on and you never tell me anything."

"It's my job to protect you," Marisol said. "I didn't want to see you hurt."

"It hurt worse, not knowing."

Did it? Marisol wasn't so sure about that. She'd spent months turning a blind eye to Lamar's activities, telling herself they were only going through a rough patch in their marriage, that time would bring them close again. When she'd learned about the gambling—and the other women and the drugs—it had been a double wound. She'd suffered the pain of his betrayal, along with the hurt of knowing she'd been deceiving herself. "I wish I could wave a magic wand and make everything better," she said. "But I can't. I know this is hard for you. It's hard for me, too. We just have to do the best we can. Tell me more about school. Isn't there anyone there who's friendly?"

Toni picked at invisible lint on her skirt. "There's this one boy. His name's Calvin."

Something in Toni's voice, some *softness*, made Marisol alert. "What's Calvin like?"

"He's a big black guy. I think maybe he plays basketball." She wrinkled her nose. "He's sort of my friend, and sort of not. He's always giving me a hard time, telling me I should smile more and be nicer to people so they'll be nice to me."

"Hmm. Do you think maybe he's right?"

"Why should I be nice to people when they're so mean to me?"

"But Calvin isn't mean."

"No. He can be really nice. We have some classes together, and we eat lunch together."

"Maybe I'll get to meet him sometime." She nudged Toni with her elbow. "Is he cute?"

"Mom!"

"Okay, I'll stop being nosy. But seriously, is there anything I can do to help? Do you want me to talk to your teachers, or buy you some new clothes so you'll fit in better?"

"Don't talk to my teachers!" This was clearly

the most mortifying thing Toni could think of. "And the clothes I have are fine." She set her mouth in a stubborn line. "We're only going to be here a little while. I'll tough it out."

Marisol patted Toni's thigh. "Good girl. And I'll try not to do anything in my dance classes to embarrass you. I imagine most of my students will be younger children, anyway."

"Mom, you can't help but embarrass me, it's what parents do." Her tone was teasing and her tears had dried, so Marisol felt hopeful. One more storm weathered. Countless more to go. All part of life with a teenager. Considering everything Toni had been through in the last year, Marisol was grateful she was doing as well as she was. If being embarrassed at the thought of her mother in a leotard was the biggest crisis the girl had to face, then Marisol would gladly tap dance down Main Street any day of the week.

Chapter Six

Toni's high school woes recalled too keenly Marisol's own turbulent years at Cedar Switch High. She knew too well that the only thing worse for a teenager than not fitting in was being made fun of by girls who thought they were better.

So when she walked through the door of Wright Construction the next morning and saw the blue-eyed blonde seated behind the desk, she thought her mind must be playing tricks on her. The woman was the very image of the cheerleader and prom queen who had tormented Marisol throughout her freshman and sophomore years. "Jessica Freeman?" she asked, shaken.

Faint lines formed on the blonde's forehead. "Marisol?" She stood and came around the corner of the desk. "Marisol Luna? I heard you were back in town."

The two women faced each other, neither of them knowing what to do with their hands. Marisol folded her arms across her chest, while Jessica made fists at her sides. "It's Jessica Wright now," she said. "I'm married to Damon Wright." She nodded toward the Wright Construction sign.

"You still look the same," Marisol said. On closer inspection, she detected a few lines on Jessica's face, and the beginning of a double chin, but overall she was remarkably the same, right down to the cut of her hair and the snug fit of her jeans.

"Oh, I've changed." Jessica gave a nervous laugh. "A lot." She moved back around the desk. "You look great. I'm, uh, I'm sorry about your husband."

"Thank you." What else could she say, though she doubted there was any real sympathy behind Jessica's comments. She pulled a folding chair closer to the desk and sat. "I need some work done at my house and my real estate agent recommended your husband."

"Oh, sure." Jessica opened a legal pad to a fresh page and picked up a pen. "Who's your agent?"

"Scott Redmond."

Jessica smiled, showing the perfect white teeth Marisol had always envied, until she'd been able to afford having her own straightened and whitened. "Scott's a great guy. I really admire the way he's put his life back together."

"Put his life back together after what?" she asked. Scott didn't look like a man with tragedy in his past, but then, she didn't really know that much about him.

"Oh, it's nothing." Jessica clicked the pen a few times. "What work did you need done?"

Marisol couldn't see any way to pursue the matter without outright prying. She'd been the victim of nosiness and gossip enough in her own life and she wasn't willing to subject anyone else to it. "I want to start giving dancing lessons at my home, so I need to convert the front room into a studio."

"What kind of dance?" Jessica asked.

"Tap and ballet to begin with. Maybe modern dance later on, if there's enough interest."

"My little girl took ballet from Mrs. Peabody before she died," Jessica said. "She's been wanting to continue her lessons, but I just don't have the time to drive her back and forth to Beeville every week."

"Maybe you'd consider enrolling her in my classes," Marisol said. "How old is she?"

"She's thirteen. Her name is Shawna." She turned a photo around that showed Jessica with a burly dark-haired man and a little blond boy and girl. The girl had her mother's blue eyes and dimpled smile.

"You have a nice family," Marisol said. The whole exchange made her uneasy. Jessica Freeman was never this nice to her. Ever.

"I guess you'll need to install mirrors," Jessica said, making notes on her pad. "And some of those dance bars. What about the floor?"

"I think there's still wood under the carpet. I'm hoping we can take out the rugs and get by without refinishing the floor. The house is for sale, so I don't know how long I'll actually be staying there."

"Oh?" Jessica continued making notes. "Are you planning to move to one of those newer houses out by the golf course? Or some of the older Victorians downtown have been restored and are really beautiful."

"I don't plan to stay in Cedar Switch." Marisol crossed her legs and hugged her purse to her stomach.

Jessica looked up, clearly surprised. "Why not? This is a great place to raise kids. You have a daughter, don't you?"

"Yes," Marisol said stiffly. Of course everyone here knew everything about her—or thought they did. The papers had laid bare almost every aspect of her life in the months leading up to and during the trial.

"I think it's so much nicer here than in Houston," Jessica continued, oblivious to Marisol's discomfort. "We don't have the pollution and traffic, and the schools are great. And now that they've built the new mall over on the west side of town, we don't have to drive an hour each way to shop."

"How much do you think the work I need done will cost?" Marisol asked.

"Oh." Jessica flushed, and focused her attention once more on the pad. "How big is the room?"

Marisol opened her purse and took out the measurements Toni had helped her with the night before. Jessica studied them, made a few more notes on her pad, then punched furiously at a calculator for several minutes. Finally she wrote down a figure, circled it, and turned the pad so that Marisol could read it. "That's time and materials. There also might be a dump fee for disposing of the old carpet and pad, but it shouldn't be more than twenty or thirty dollars."

Marisol nodded. The fee was lower than she'd expected, another reminder that she was no longer living in pricey River Oaks. "That sounds good. When do you think he can start?"

"I'm not sure, but maybe as soon as next week."

"Good. How much do you want as a deposit?"

"Oh, a hundred dollars is fine now. Damon will collect more when he's been over there and seen exactly what materials he'll need."

Marisol wrote the check and handed it over, then stood. "My number's on there. Your husband can call and arrange a time to stop by and see the place."

"Thanks." Jessica put the check in a drawer, then stood also. "It was great seeing you again," she said.

Marisol knew she was supposed to agree, but she couldn't bring the lie to her lips. "I'd better go," she said instead, and turned toward the door.

"Marisol, wait." Jessica hurried after her.

"It's almost time for me to close up for lunch," she said. "Why don't we go get a sandwich somewhere and talk?"

"What do the two of us have to talk about?" Marisol asked coldly.

Jessica flushed, but she didn't back down. "Actually, a lot," she said. She took her purse from a hook by the door. "Come on. I'll buy."

Feeling as if she'd stepped into an alternate reality, Marisol followed her former enemy out the door and down the sidewalk to a small blue house. Nettie's Tearoom and Antiques, proclaimed the sign in the yard.

"Nettie has good chicken salad and cookies," Jessica said, leading the way up the steps. "And fancy teas and coffee drinks, too."

The women ordered chicken salad and iced tea, then faced each other across the table. "What did you want to talk about?" Marisol asked warily.

Jessica sipped her tea, then set the glass aside and wiped her hands on a pink linen napkin. "I wanted to ask you to forgive me for being such a bitch in high school," she said.

Marisol caught her breath. "I...what brought this on?"

Anguish distorted Jessica's pretty face. "I've made a lot of mistakes in my life, but I'm trying hard to make up for them now. When I saw you'd moved back to town, I decided to find a way to tell you how sorry I was. I was awful to you when we were girls. I know nothing I do now can make up for that, but I'm hoping you'll find it in yourself to forgive me."

Marisol certainly knew about mistakes, having made more than her share. But being on the giving end of absolution was more difficult than she'd anticipated. She hesitated, avoiding Jessica's gaze, the silence stretching between them. "All right," she said finally. "I—I forgive you. I guess both of us are different people than we were back then."

"Yes, I guess we are." Jessica's smile was bright, but there was sadness behind the radiance.

The waitress brought their salads and Marisol picked up a fork to eat. "You probably know all about me from the papers," she said. "But what have you been up to since high school?"

"I married Danny Westover right after graduation. That was mistake number one."

"What did Danny end up doing?" The handsome quarterback had been the big man on campus back then. He and Jessica were class royalty.

"He spent the summer before college working

at his dad's used car lot and partying with all his friends. He was drunk and drag racing out on County Line Road one weekend and wrecked his car. Tore up his leg, so there went his football scholarship." Jessica scooped chicken salad onto a cracker and contemplated it. "I should have known right then nothing good was going to come of staying with him, but I thought getting married would solve all our problems, so that's what we did. He went to work for his dad and I got a job at the county courthouse and we were going to live happily ever after." She snorted, then bit down hard on the cracker.

"Let me guess," Marisol said. "He kept drinking and partying."

Jessica nodded. "And I kept making excuses for him, telling myself he was just sowing his wild oats and that he'd grow up and settle down. I wanted to have a baby, but he kept saying he wasn't ready. Finally, I told him I was tired of waiting and I got pregnant with Shawna. That was another mistake. Not having Shawna, but thinking a baby would fix all our problems."

"You're not the first woman who's thought that," Marisol said.

"No, and not the last, I'm sure. Our boy, Nathan, came along two years later. By then I was pretty unhappy with my marriage, but thought I should tough it out for the sake of my kids."

"What happened to change your thinking?"

"The big C." She took a long drink of tea, the words hanging in the air between them. "I was still nursing Nathan when I felt a lump in my breast. It turned out to be cancer. Stage Two. I had a mastectomy, went through chemo and radiation. Lost all my hair and looked and felt like hell." She laughed, a jarring contrast to the grim picture her words painted. "I remember one Friday night, I was leaning over the toilet puking up my guts, with Nathan clinging to my hip, crying, while Shawna sat in the bathtub, wailing that she was cold, and Danny came in smelling like a barroom floor and asked me why there wasn't any dinner on the table." She shook her head. "I didn't even have the energy to be angry with him. I just sat there, thinking, why am I staying in this hell when I'm still alive and can do something about it?"

She stabbed at her salad again. Marisol's admiration grew as her words sank in. "What did you do?" she prompted.

"As soon as my last treatment was done I called up a lawyer and filed for divorce. Danny didn't even fight it. And then I spent a lot of time thinking about what I really wanted in life. I realized I'd brought a lot of my problems on myself. Not the cancer, but my sorry marriage and everything that went with that." She grimaced. "And I realized I hadn't been a very nice person a lot of the time. I started going to church and to Al-Anon. I figured I'd been given a second chance and I wanted to get things right this time."

Could a person really transform her life completely through sheer willpower? Marisol wondered. "When did you meet your new husband?" she asked.

"I met Damon at church. We dated for a year and he got to know the kids. He's really good with them." She blushed. "Lately, we've been talking about having a baby together. I hope we can."

"I always thought I'd like to have another child," Marisol said, feeling wistful. "But it never happened."

"You're still young enough," Jessica said. "Women are having babies into their forties all the time these days."

"Last I checked, you still need a man for that."

"Well, yeah, but there are still a few good ones left." She gave Marisol a sly look. "I hear

Scott Redmond just broke up with his girl-friend."

Marisol almost choked on her iced tea. She coughed, and wiped her mouth. "She was upset about his picture in the paper with me. I'm sure they'll be back together soon."

"I don't think so." Jessica shook her head. "Tiffany's a nice girl, but I never thought she was right for Scott. She sort of threw herself at him when he was in a vulnerable place and he's too nice a guy to dump her. But now that she's gone, I don't think he'll be quick to take her back."

What had happened to make Scott vulnerable? *None of your business,* she reminded herself. "I'm sure he's a nice guy, but I'm not interested in getting involved with anyone," she said. Having everyone think so would make it easier to hide an affair if she and Scott did decide to indulge in a temporary fling.

"I can respect that. I felt the same way for a long time after Danny and I split." Jessica finished the last of her salad and pushed her plate aside. "So you're opening a dance studio. What made you decide to do that? Did you teach dance in Houston?"

"No. I took dance classes, though, so I'm confident I can teach." She traced a drop of condensation down the side of her glass with the tip of her finger. "Frankly, I need the money. The trial left me pretty broke and no one in town will give me a job after the fiasco with the photographer and the reporter at the café."

Jessica nodded sympathetically. "I'll sign up Shawna, and I'll tell all the other mothers I know."

"Thanks. As soon as we finish eating, I'm headed to the copy shop to have some flyers made to put up around town, and I thought I'd advertise in the paper."

"I'm sure you can get a lot of Mrs. Peabody's former students."

"I hope so. I was sad to hear she'd died."

"She was a great woman, and the children loved her. Last year after the recital they pooled their money and bought her this big box of fancy chocolates, because she'd told them once she loved chocolate."

"Did she still have her recitals at the old hotel?" Marisol asked. "I hear it's slated to be torn down."

"Last year was the last one there. Marcus Henry bought the building shortly afterward and shut it up."

"I can't believe he's going to tear down such

a beautiful, historical place," Marisol said. "To put in loft apartments."

"I know." Jessica nodded. "It's like putting a dairy farm in the middle of downtown Houston—completely out of place. But he thinks he can sell them to people with more money than sense, I guess."

"There are a few of those around," Marisol agreed. "Still, I've been thinking of trying to find a way to save the hotel. Maybe have it restored." The idea had come to her slowly. Of course, she wouldn't be around to really care if the hotel was still there or not, but she liked the idea of doing something to make sure people here didn't forget her. Something good that would be one more way of thumbing her nose at those who'd despised her.

"How are you going to do that?" Jessica asked.

"I thought I'd start by talking to Mr. Henry."

Jessica snorted again. "Unless you've got the money to buy the hotel—at his price—I don't think you'll get very far. Some environmental group tried to stop him from building his golf course last year. They lasted about as long as snowflakes in June."

"If we could get the property declared a historic landmark, he wouldn't be able to tear it down," Marisol said.

"Could you do that?"

"I've been on committees where it was done," she said. "There's a lot of paperwork involved, but it can happen, if enough people are interested."

Jessica giggled. "Count me in. I'd love it if somebody took Marcus Henry down a peg or two." She leaned over the table and spoke in a low voice. "Damon and some of the other local contractors approached him about giving them the contracts for new construction at his new subdivision and he told them he could save more money by bringing in crews of illegal aliens from Houston and Dallas. I never saw Damon so mad."

"Do you think there are others in town who might be interested?" Marisol asked.

"I'm sure of it."

"Even if they know I'm involved?" Marisol avoided looking at Jessica while she waited for the answer to her question.

"They'll want to join us *because* you're involved," Jessica said. "It's not every day we have a celebrity in town."

"It's not as if I'm a movie star." Marisol kept

her voice low. "People only know me because I was accused of murdering my husband."

"It doesn't take more than that to get folks around here excited." She laughed at Marisol's horrified expression. "Relax, I'm just teasing. We probably will get a few people who show up just to get a look at you, but once they see you're serious about doing this, they'll appreciate the effort."

"I hope so." She wasn't so sure. Maybe Jessica's determination to turn over a new leaf in her own life gave her an overly generous view of everyone else's motives.

"So what do you say?" Jessica held up her glass of iced tea. "Friends?"

Jessica Freeman and Marisol Luna, friends? Two hours ago, Marisol would have said it could never happen. Yet she couldn't remember the last time she'd felt so relaxed with another woman. So…hopeful. "I'm not really planning on staying in town that much longer," she said.

"Where you're going will have telephones and internet, right?" Jessica said. "Besides, I'll give you someone to eat lunch with and I promise to dish the latest gossip until you do move on."

Marisol lifted her glass. "Friends," she said.

The glasses clinked and the women drank, smiling at each other across the table.

Scott stood in his kitchen, trying to decide between frozen pizza and frozen burritos for dinner, when the doorbell rang. He tossed both boxes in the sink, wiped his hands on a dish towel, and went to answer the summons. Maybe his dad was stopping by to invite him to dinner.

He glanced through the wavy diamond pane at the top center of the door and couldn't breathe as he recognized the fall of long dark hair framing the oval face. He steadied himself with one hand against the wall as the bell rang again. Somehow he managed to jerk open the door. Yes, it really was her standing there, her lush lips, shiny with pink lip gloss, turned up at the corners in a suggestion of a smile. "Marisol, is something wrong?"

She arched one eyebrow. "Is that how you see me—as some damsel in distress always needing rescuing?"

"Of course not." He saw her as a mesmerizing, mysterious woman who kept him teetering between confidence and doubt. "Come in." He stepped back to allow her to pass. "It's good to see you."

"I don't blame you if you do think I need

rescuing," she said. "I've had a knack for getting into situations I couldn't get out of without help. Or rather, I thought some man would help me, but they seldom did."

Why was she telling him this? And why was she even here? She walked past him into the room, hips swaying in a formfitting tropical-print dress. His gaze traveled from those hips down her legs to bright red shoes with four-inch heels and delicate ankle straps. Shoes that sent a definite message. "Can I get you a drink?" he asked. He no longer drank, but he thought he might have some wine in the house that Tiffany had brought once.

"No, thank you." She walked to the sofa. "Why don't we sit down?"

"All right." He lowered himself into a recliner, his eyes fixed on her. She sat on the end of the couch closest to him. "Toni's spending the night with Jessica Wright's daughter," she said. "They're close to the same age and Jessica and I thought it would be good if they got to know each other better. Jessica's daughter, Shawna, goes to a private Baptist school here in town."

"Jessica and Damon are good people," Scott said. They'd remained friends with him after others had deserted him. He leaned forward, elbows on his knees. "Marisol, what are you *doing* here?"

"Can't you guess?"

"I could guess a lot of things. But why don't you tell me?"

"All right." She squared her shoulders and looked him in the eye. "You and I are obviously attracted to each other, so I thought it was time we did something about it."

He opened his mouth, but no words came out.

"You *are* attracted to me, aren't you?" she asked.

"Yes." He cleared his throat and tried to collect his wits. The last thing he wanted was to look like some eager schoolboy, though too often that's how she made him feel. Further proof he was in over his head here. "What, exactly, are you suggesting?"

"I realize you just broke up with a woman," she said. "You probably aren't interested in anything long-term right now. Neither am I. I don't plan on being here very many months, but while I'm here I don't see why we couldn't enjoy ourselves."

"Have an affair?"

"Yes." She seemed pleased that he'd finally caught on. "We'd have to be absolutely discreet, of course. I don't want Toni knowing. And I wouldn't want to hurt your reputation."

"Hurt my reputation?" A bark of laughter escaped him. "I seriously doubt anything you do could hurt my reputation."

She frowned. "Everyone I've spoken with speaks very highly of you. After all, your father is one of the most respected men in town."

"Yes, he is." Too bad Scott had been such a disappointment. Not that he didn't still have friends here, but he couldn't help thinking they pitied him as much as anything. "You're not worried about *your* reputation?" he asked.

She shrugged. "There are plenty of people here who already think the worst of me. Nothing I do is going to change their minds. As for the rest… I don't intend for them to ever know."

"And when you leave town, we just say goodbye, it's been great." He told himself he could handle this. It would be for the best, really.

"I hope it will have been great." Her eyes sparkled with delight.

"Oh, it will be." He was out of his chair, gathering her into his arms before she could say anything else. God help him, he might be making the biggest mistake of his life, but he wasn't going to say no to the chance to be with her, however briefly.

Chapter Seven

They kissed with the hunger of lovers long-parted, bodies pressed together, hands groping, eyes tightly closed, as if to shut out every other sense and sensation but the feel of each other. They fell back on the sofa, still entwined.

"Open your eyes," he coaxed.

She did so, and stared into eyes the same dark gray-blue as storm clouds. He cradled her cheek in his palm, his skin warm and rough against hers. "When I was a boy I was sure you were the most beautiful girl I'd ever seen," he said. "But that girl was nothing compared to the woman you are now."

"You should have seen me ten years ago,"

she said, suddenly nervous under the intensity of his gaze.

"No. There's a beauty inside you that needed time to develop." He scooted up, the length of his body covering hers. "Or I needed to be older to appreciate it."

All nervousness vanished as his arms encircled her once more and they kissed again, replaced by an eagerness that made her bold. She teased him with her tongue and he responded in kind, exploring the sensitive nerve endings of lips and mouth until every part of her was alive with wanting him.

She slid her hands beneath his shirt, smoothing her palms across the flat plane of his stomach and the hard muscle of his chest, feeling the steady, strong beat of his heart beneath her fingers. She held her hands there, scarcely breathing as he unfastened her blouse, his fingers fumbling with the buttons, biting one lip as he focused on the task.

But at last the two halves of fabric fell away, and with one expert twist he released the front clasp of her bra.

"What are you smiling about?" he asked.

She hadn't realized until that moment that she was smiling. "I was thinking this is going to be a lot better than it would have been when we were kids," she said.

"I may have learned a few things since then," he said, gently pushing aside her hands and lowering his head to her breast.

She was like a paralytic coming back to life, every touch awakening her to new sensations. It had been so long since she'd allowed herself to really *feel* anything. She'd survived the past year by remaining mostly numb, but all that vanished as Scott lavished her body with kisses and caresses.

She wanted to touch him, too, to feel the soft furring of hair on his chest over taut muscle, to seek out the flat brown nipples and taste the faintly salty sweat at the base of his throat. They cast clothing aside without a thought to where it landed, and twined in each other's arms and legs with the abandon of lovers for whom there is no past or present, only this heated moment.

He rolled, pulling her on top of him, and smiled up at her as she straddled him. "I've got you where I want you now," she teased, reaching down to stroke his erection. The heat and hardness of it made her breathless with wanting him.

His eyes lost focus and she recognized the

effort it took for him to speak. "I'm all yours. I have been since the day you walked into my office."

"Oh, you have, have you?" Her teasing tone hid how much his words unsettled her. What did it mean that his attraction had been instantaneous, while hers had unfolded more slowly?

His expression sobered. "I knew what I wanted," he said. "But you had to want it too."

The idea that he had spent all this time thinking about her—*wanting* her—made her temperature shoot up another few degrees. She lay down on top of him, her breasts pressed to his chest, his erection nuzzling her stomach. "I want you, too," she said. She squirmed, enjoying the way his eyes lost focus and his mouth went slack.

Then, in one swift move, he rolled her over and pinned her beneath him. She giggled and pretended to fight him, while he caressed her hip and studied her face. "Do you really think you're ready for me?" he teased.

She was more than ready. Except...

"What is it?" he asked. "Why are you looking at me that way?"

She swallowed hard. "I'm not on any kind of birth control," she said. "And this really wouldn't be a good time to get pregnant."

"I can take care of that." He rolled off of her and left the room, returning in a moment with a familiar foil packet. Of course, he'd had a girlfriend. He hadn't been living a celibate life—not like her.

When he reached for her once more she pulled him down on top of her, and spread her legs wide, inviting him in—into her body, and into the empty spaces in her heart that had been vacant for too long.

Every movement and maneuver revealed new discoveries, about each other and about themselves. When she wrapped her legs around him, she realized part of her never wanted him to leave her again. And when he caressed her hip and smoothed his hand around to her bottom it was with the possessiveness of a man who has found the one thing he has spent years searching for.

Then their need drove out coherent thought, and passion overtook patience. His thrusts became harder, her cries more insistent, her body arched beneath him as she shuddered with her climax, eyes squeezed shut against the white light exploding within her.

All light had faded from the room as they lay, still entwined on the sofa. Scott had dragged an afghan over them against the air-conditioned chill.

"What would you normally be doing on a Friday night?" she asked him. "Would you go over to Tiffany's, or would she come here?" She hated the jealousy that pinched at her at the thought of him with another woman, but she couldn't help herself.

"I don't want to talk about Tiffany," he said, settling more firmly against her.

He was a gentleman. She should have been comforted by this knowledge. He wouldn't kiss and tell. But the strangeness of their situation unsettled her. She'd thought it would be easy to have sex with him without any emotional attachment. After the way Lamar had hurt her, she would have said she wasn't even capable of caring what any man thought or felt. And yet...

"You haven't asked anything about Lamar," she said.

"I don't want to know."

"Lamar wanted to know everything. Every man I'd ever dated, much less slept with. Everything I thought and felt." At the time, she'd been flattered by his desire to know her so completely. Only later had she realized how little he'd revealed of himself.

"It doesn't matter," Scott said. "I don't care

what you've done before. I only want to enjoy now."

"That's exactly what we should do. We should enjoy now." She closed her eyes, and let herself drift in this unfamiliar sated euphoria.

But the peace was shattered by the marimba rhythm from her phone. "I'd better get that," she said, as she climbed over Scott and lunged for the purse she'd dropped beside the sofa. "Hello?"

"Mom, where are you?" Toni's voice was plaintive. "I called the house and you weren't there."

"I had some errands to run. What do you need?"

"I wanted to know if it was okay if I go to the pool with Shawna. Jessica said I needed to ask you."

"All right. Do you want me to bring you your bathing suit?"

"That's okay. Shawna has one I can borrow. We're the same size."

"Are you having a good time?"

"Yeah. It's okay. Are you going to be okay, spending the night by yourself?"

A lump rose in Marisol's throat. "I'll be okay," she said.

"What are you going to do?"

"I'll probably just watch some TV." And think about the incredible sex she'd had with Scott. "You have fun at the pool," she said. "I'll pick you up about ten tomorrow. I thought we could check out the mall."

"Okay."

She folded the phone and replaced it in her purse. "Everything okay?" Scott asked.

She nodded. "Toni wanted permission to go swimming. But I think she wanted to make sure I was okay, too."

"It must have been tough on her, those months when you were in jail. Hard for you, too, of course."

"It was." She gathered her clothes and put them on.

Scott slipped on his jeans, but didn't bother with a shirt. "Do you want to stay for supper?" he asked. "I've got a frozen pizza."

"Thanks, but I'd better go home. In case Toni calls again." She smoothed her hair with her hands and picked up her purse. "If it's okay with you, I'll go out the back door."

"Where did you park?"

"At the grocery store around the block. I didn't think it would be a good idea if anyone saw my car parked here too long."

He nodded. "It's getting late. Let me walk you to the store."

"No, I'll be fine. I'm a city girl, remember? I can look after myself."

She'd expected to feel exhilarated after being with him—energized by not only the sex, but the knowledge that she'd made the first move, not a man. She'd decided to do something to take care of her own needs, without permission or persuasion from anyone else.

But her newfound independence didn't feel as great as she'd anticipated it would. More than once on the walk to her car, she was tempted to turn around and go back to Scott's warm arms. Frozen pizza with a loving man seemed far better than scrambled eggs in her own lonely kitchen. She fought the temptation. She was through with thinking men could make her happy. She had to find her way past the pain and loneliness on her own. Scott was a pleasant pastime, but she wouldn't allow him to be anything more.

Marisol decided to spend Sunday painting the front room before Damon and his crew started work on Monday morning. "You can help, too," she told Toni as the two of them searched the aisles of the local big box hardware store for the right shade of white paint.

"Can I paint my bedroom, too?" Toni asked.

"I don't know," Marisol said. "What color do you want?"

Toni made a face. "Any color but pink."

"I don't know if we'll have time to paint the living room and the bedroom, too," Marisol said.

"Calvin said he'd come over and help me." Toni's voice was overly casual, her eyes fixed firmly on a display of paint cans.

Marisol bit back a smile. This might be her best chance to meet the mysterious Calvin. "All right then. Pick out a couple of gallons, but nothing too dark."

Toni chose a soft lavender, while Marisol selected a five-gallon bucket of off-white. She added brushes, rollers, spackle, gloves, tape and drop cloths and headed for the checkout counter. Thank goodness Jessica—and Calvin— were coming to help. Otherwise, she might never get it all done.

When she answered the doorbell the next morning, however, she found not only Jessica, but Scott. Dressed in ripped jeans and a faded T-shirt that stretched tight over his chest and shoulders, his brown hair covered by a Houston Astros cap, he radiated masculine energy. Her mind immediately flashed a picture of him, naked, and heat flooded her. She took a step back, avoiding looking at him, fearful she would give too much away.

"I hope you don't mind I accepted Scott's offer to help," Jessica said, eyes twinkling with mischief. "I thought it might be nice to have some muscle on this job, and Damon's tied up with a remodel on the other side of town and the kids are with their dad." She grinned and sashayed past Marisol, who only then risked another look at Scott.

"Consider this part of my services as your listing agent," he said, his eyes telegraphing another message entirely. He was remembering Friday night, too, she was sure. And perhaps, like her, wondering when they'd be able to be alone again.

"Do you do this for all your clients?" she asked, keeping up her pretense of indifference.

"Only very special ones." His voice was soft, smooth as warm honey, and she felt her knees go wobbly as he looked into her eyes.

She looked away and opened the door wider. "Come on in," she said. "You can do the ceiling." It was the worst job, but hey, he was the tallest, and maybe that assignment would allow her to keep some physical distance between them and figure out how to handle herself in public around this man who'd sent her long-dormant libido into overdrive.

"What is *he* doing here?" Toni asked. Her mouth was pinched, her nose wrinkled as if she'd smelled something foul.

"Scott came to help," Marisol said. "He's our friend."

"He's not my friend." She snatched up a roll of tape and fled the room.

"Did I do something wrong?" Scott asked.

"I think Toni's having a hard time imagining any other man in her mom's life, now that her dad is gone," Jessica said.

Marisol opened her mouth to protest that Scott was not *in* her life. At least, not openly. But she decided her protests would only add to any suspicions Jessica might have. "She needs to get used to me having all kinds of new friends," she said. "I'll talk to her later. Right now, we have work to do."

Scott volunteered to mix the paint while she and Jessica taped the trim. They'd just started work when the doorbell rang again. "I'll get it," Toni called, running from her room. She opened the door to admit a tall young man with coffee colored skin and kind eyes.

"Mom, this is Calvin Anderson," Toni said, hovering between them like a moth afraid to light.

"Hello, Mrs. Dixon," he said, shaking her hand. She didn't bother to correct him on the name. It was Toni's name, so Marisol was perfectly willing to answer to it. She'd only changed it in hopes of keeping a lower public profile.

"My room's back here," Toni said, tugging him toward the hallway.

Calvin nodded at the adults, then followed Toni out of the room.

"He's cute," Jessica said, sidling up to Marisol.

"Do you know anything about him?" Marisol asked.

"I think his father works for the Sheriff's Department."

Marisol nodded, unsure how she felt about this information. After all, her own recent interactions with law enforcement hadn't been entirely pleasant. Still, from everything Toni had told her, he seemed like a nice young man, and she was glad Toni had a friend.

Soon the throb of music from down the hall blocked any effort Marisol might have made to eavesdrop on the teens. She'd make it a point

to stop by every so often to check on the progress of the painting. Not that she didn't trust
her daughter, but if she didn't make an appearance, what would Toni have to roll her eyes and
complain about?

Marisol and Jessica continued taping while
Scott started on the ceiling. Though he didn't
say a word, Marisol was constantly aware of
his presence, filling the room and crowding
against her. She imagined he was watching
her, yet every time she turned around he was
focused on his work.

By the same token, she had to fight to keep
from staring at him as he stretched up to paint
the ceiling. He wasn't as tall as Lamar had
been—few people were—but she guessed he
was at least six feet, and he had strong back
and shoulders. And a nice butt.

"What are you grinning about?" Jessica
nudged her in the side.

"I'm thinking about my dance classes," she
lied, stretching tape along the molding near the
floor. "I can't wait to get my first students."

"Uh-huh." Jessica held out her hand. "I need
some more tape." She glanced over her shoulder at Scott, then leaned closer and whispered.
"I told you he was a great guy—and not bad-
looking either."

"Jessica, don't."

"Don't what?"

"Don't play matchmaker. I'm not interested." Not in the way Jessica wanted her to be— interested in happily-ever-after and 'til-death-do-us-part.

"I never said anything about you going out with him. But a person can't have too many friends, you know."

Marisol shook her head.

"What?" Jessica poked her again.

"Do you really think a man and a woman can be just friends?" she asked.

"As a matter of fact, I do. Scott and I are friends."

"That's because you're already happily married. It's different between two single people."

"Oh, you mean the sex thing. I didn't figure it made any difference with you, since you're *not interested*."

"What are you two whispering about over there?" Scott interrupted them. "I'm starting to feel paranoid."

"Marisol was just telling me how the two of you can't be friends because of sex," Jessica said.

She laughed and jumped out of the way as

Marisol lunged toward her. "You are such a troublemaker," Marisol said, her face burning.

Scott wisely chose not to comment on the subject, though his cheeks, too, were more flushed than usual. He turned back to his painting, but S-E-X might as well have been painted in yard-high letters on the wall for all Marisol could get her mind off the subject now. Her thoughts were filled with memories of Friday evening, of his arms around her and his lips on hers, of him filling her and surrounding her and making her feel more whole than she had in a very long time.

The truth was, Scott was the first man she'd met in over a year with whom she hadn't had something of an adversarial relationship. Even the team of lawyers who had defended her during her murder trial had spent much of their time grilling her, preparing her for the prosecution's tactics. The law enforcement officers, jailers and reporters who had been part of her daily life for months had approached her with, at the most, cold courtesy.

So maybe it wasn't so unusual to think she'd react positively to the first man who showed her some kindness. Hers was simply the normal response of a healthy woman. It proved that part of her hadn't been killed off by her ordeal, but it didn't mean she was really *emotionally* involved with him.

The thought helped her relax, and by the time she and Jessica had finished taping all the trim she accepted Scott's help attaching an extension pole to the roller with hardly a flutter.

The Marisol Scott had held in his mind over the years had been the teenage version—beautiful and distant, full of angry energy and prickly bravado, overlaying a sadness that hinted at some pain in her life he could never touch.

The woman he knew today carried that same sadness, but much of the anger was gone, replaced by a watchful strength and stillness. Friday night had been the incredible fulfillment of a dream, but it had shown him how vulnerable he was to letting himself go too far with her. She'd made it clear she was using him for a temporary affair and he had no further claims on her. He couldn't allow himself to think otherwise.

Yet, when he was with her he felt edgy and reckless, things he hadn't allowed himself to feel since he'd emerged from rehab. The part of him that urged caution was getting harder and harder to hear, the longer he stayed in her presence.

So when she struggled to manipulate the paint roller with its long-handled pole, he stepped forward to help her, and let his hand linger on her arm, enjoying the heat of her bare skin against his palm. She stepped away after a moment, eyes downcast, cheeks flushed.

Right. He needed to slow down and cool things off. They were supposed to be discreet, keeping their sexual relationship a secret from everyone. He stepped away from her and picked up another roller. "Do you have any students signed up for classes yet?" he asked.

"Jessica's daughter, and a couple of people who responded to the flyers I distributed around town. I paid for an ad to run in the local paper this week, so I'm hoping to pick up more."

"I meant to tell you, I've talked to some other mothers and they're all interested," Jessica said. "They should be calling you soon."

"If I come across any clients with kids, I'll be sure to let them know," Scott said.

"Thanks."

With that one word and smile his attempt at calm and coolness evaporated. He forced himself to look away, but his heart still thudded in his chest.

The tinny melody of a fanfare ringtone sounded. Jessica set aside her roller. "That's mine," she said as she lunged for her purse.

The other two went back to work, though it was impossible not to listen to Jessica's side of the conversation. "Hello?... Yes. What?... Oh, no!... I'll be right there."

"Is everything okay?" Marisol asked when Jessica had hung up.

"Danny's youngest little boy fell out of a tree and broke his arm," she said, digging her keys out of a side pocket of her purse. "Apparently, he can't handle that and his other children too, so I have to meet him at the hospital and get my kids. I'm sorry."

"It's okay," Marisol reassured her. "We're almost finished here, anyway."

"I'll call you later." Jessica hugged Marisol, waved goodbye to Scott and hurried out the door.

Scott was acutely aware that now he and Marisol were alone, except for the two young people in the next room, the music blaring from the teens' radio separating them from the adults like a wall. "Why don't I start on the brush work and you finish up with the roller?" Marisol said.

How did she do it? She was as cool and indifferent as if they were scarcely above strangers, yet he felt on fire, struggling to keep from staring at her, or from pulling her to him.

"Sure." He watched as she knelt and added paint to a small tray. He had a hundred questions he wanted to ask her, questions there had been no time for Friday night. He'd been honest when he told her he didn't want to know about Lamar, but after she'd left, he'd thought of a million other things he did want to know, about her life since she'd left Cedar Switch, about her plans for the future. But where to begin?

"Scott, have you been married before?"

The question startled him. He stared at her. "No. Did you think I had?"

She shrugged. "I wondered." She stroked a narrow line of paint along the taped molding. "Jessica said something about you putting your life back together and I thought…maybe a divorce, or a death."

So that was it. He supposed he shouldn't have been surprised. Practically everyone in town knew his story, and sooner or later someone would tell her. He turned back to his painting, searching for the right words. "I was in rehab last year," he said. "Drugs. I screwed up pretty bad, but I'm over that now." He'd leave out the loss of his job, threat of jail time, the disgrace to his family and his own lingering anxiety. He could only reveal one shame at a time.

"Oh." She was silent, the throb of rock music from the other room providing a background for their thoughts. "That must have been tough," she said after a moment. She glanced at him. "I think it takes a strong person to get through something like that."

Or a weak one to get into it in the first place, he thought. "You'd know a thing or two about being strong," he said. "I followed the coverage of the trial. They put you through a lot, but you never broke down."

"I never broke down in public."

The idea of what she must have suffered in private tore at him, but he couldn't come up with any way to say this without risking her thinking he pitied her. Marisol didn't strike him as a woman who welcomed pity.

She stood and stretched, back arched, breasts thrust forward in a way that left his mouth dry. He forced his eyes back to the wall in front on him. "How did you meet Lamar?" he asked. So maybe he'd lied before. He *did* want to know about her late husband. To discover the thing in him that had drew and held her. "Does it bother you to talk about him?"

"No, it doesn't bother me." She walked over to the paint cans and refilled her tray. "We met at a club where I was working as a cocktail waitress. He came in with a group of friends. He flirted and he asked me out—and we stayed together for almost seventeen years."

"Were the things that came out at the trial about him a surprise to you?"

"Yes." She looked at him, head tilted back, the hardness of her expression a sharp contrast to the soft curls falling around her shoulders. "I realized the man I'd lived with for all those years was a stranger to me." She looked away again. "I don't know if that's the kind of thing a person can ever get over completely."

He wanted to put his hand on her shoulder, to comfort her, but again he worried she'd interpret his actions the wrong way. "I think something like that shapes who you are," he said after a moment, setting aside the paint roller. "The way my experience with addiction shaped me. It changes us, but it's only part of us, not the whole."

She returned to her painting, stroking the brush carefully alongside the trim, filling in the bare spot next to the area he'd painted with the roller. "When I left this town, I had a pretty bad reputation, you know," she said.

"I know." He picked up the roller again and started on the last bare patch of wall. "I watched you that day, when you jumped off the bridge," he said after a long moment.

She glanced toward the hallway, but the music still pounded. Over it came the sound of teenage laughter. She looked back at him. "I was really angry that day," she said. "I wanted to show everyone I didn't care what they thought of me."

"I thought you were the most beautiful thing I'd ever seen. Not just because you were naked." He smiled. "Though you are beautiful. But I also saw how brave you were. How daring."

"I didn't feel very beautiful inside. I hated my life and wanted it to be different." She set aside the brush and tray and wiped her hands on a rag. "You know I left town because of my stepfather."

"I know." Harlan Davies had been one of the most prominent men in town; it was a minor scandal when he married his Hispanic maid and brought her and her daughter to live in this house. "You know, I used to ride by here on my bicycle all the time, even after you left, hoping you might come back to visit and I'd see you."

She smiled. "You had a crush on me?"

He laughed. "Yeah. After all, you were the mysterious older woman."

"Not that much older." She shook her head, the smile gone. "I never came back. Not for twenty years."

"Why not?"

"Stupidity. Pride. I wish I could go back and change that, but it's too late now." She squeezed her eyes shut and swallowed hard. "We always think we have more time. And then my mother died and I realized my time had passed."

"I'm glad you're back now."

"Yeah, well, only because I didn't have a choice. As soon as you find a buyer for this place, I'm moving on."

"Have you thought about staying?" Talk about going out on a limb. "It's not a bad place to raise a kid. You have friends here, and you'll have dance students."

"There are too many memories here. Not good ones."

"So make some new memories." He set down the roller and moved closer to her. "I'd like it if you stayed." There. He'd said it. He held his breath, waiting for her answer.

Her eyes met his, calm and clear. "I meant what I said before. I'm not interested in a long-term relationship. I'm not ready to let another man into my life that way. I don't know if I ever will be."

He nodded. He'd agreed to accept their affair on her terms, but that didn't mean he had to like it. "Maybe you'll change your mind one day, but until then, I'm here." He took her hand in his, his large fingers laced with her slender ones. "I've been dying for one moment alone with you. You've felt it, haven't you?"

She said nothing, though the longing in her eyes answered for her.

He leaned down and brought his lips to hers, holding them there for a moment, waiting for her to draw away. She stiffened, then relaxed against him, her free hand reaching up to touch his throat, a feather-soft caress that was his undoing. He drew her to him and deepened the kiss, savoring the heat and taste of her with the tenderness of a man in a dream, who has found great treasure but can't quite believe it's his.

She pulled away first, and reluctantly he released her. She stared at him, her eyes dark and shining. "This is a bad idea," she said softly.

"It's the best one I can think of," he said, and leaned in to kiss her again, but she pressed her hand to his chest, holding him off.

"Toni is in the next room. You'd better go," she said, but a smile pulled at the corners of her mouth and lingered in her eyes, so he accepted the order with good grace and stepped away.

"I should stay and help you clean up," he said.

"The kids can help me. Right now I can't think with you here in the house."

"That might not be such a bad thing."

She sent him a pleading look and he nodded. "All right. I'll go for now," he said. "But I'll be back."

He felt as if his feet scarcely touched the ground on the way to his car. As he pulled onto the street, he looked back at the house, hoping he might see her at the window, but she wasn't there. He thought of the times he'd ridden his bicycle past here as a kid, hoping for a glimpse of her, and chuckled to himself. Maybe he hadn't changed so much after all.

Chapter Eight

Marisol threw herself into working on her dance studio and tried not to think too much about Scott. Yes, they'd had some wonderful sex and an amazing stolen kiss, but that hadn't meant anything more than that she was finally emerging from the numb state she'd been in since Lamar's death. Scott was a sexy, good-looking man and she'd responded as any woman would.

Still, that didn't mean she was ready to let him into her life as more than a physical diversion. She didn't want to ever need a man that way again.

If she needed any reminders why, all she

had to do was look around this house, and re-member the man who had originally brought her here—Harlan Davies. Though she'd re-sented him from the first for intruding on the cozy life she enjoyed with her mother, for a time she'd entertained fantasies of him being the dad she'd never had. A man who would always look out for her, love her and protect her the way she'd never been loved and pro-tected before.

She shuddered to think how badly that had turned out. Not only had Harlan not protected her, but her mother had stopped being there for her as well.

By the time Lamar had come along, she was sure she'd become a better judge of people. He'd offered her a good life, and she'd fallen into it like falling onto a feather bed. Only af-terward, sitting alone in a jail cell, had she re-alized how much of herself she'd exchanged for the comfort she'd been offered. Every time she'd turned a deaf ear to rumors of his af-fairs, or ignored her own suspicions about his more undesirable friends, she'd lost a little bit of herself.

She needed time to regain her confidence and self-respect. She hoped giving these dance classes would help. She loved dancing, but had all but given it up in the past few years. Now, as she waited for her first class to begin, she spent hours reviewing dance videos, practicing her moves and designing lessons. It felt good to focus on something besides her fears of what the future might bring.

True to his word, Jessica's husband transformed Marisol's living room into a dance studio in only a couple of days. Marisol hung long drapes to block the front windows and polished the floors—which, fortunately, had been in good shape once the carpet had been lifted—and newly installed mirrors until they shone in the glow of the new track lighting. She found framed Degas prints of ballerinas at a local thrift store and hung these on one wall, and installed a stereo on a small shelf in the corner. Luna School of Dance was ready for business.

When she wasn't dancing, Marisol turned her attention to the Palace Hotel. She became more determined than ever to save it from being torn down. She'd show the townspeople how wrong they were to let something so fine and beautiful be destroyed—and how wrong they'd been about her. She wasn't just an idle socialite or an accused murderess or the wild girl they'd once thought they knew. She was a strong woman who could accomplish things.

She could stand up to the man none of them were willing to confront.

She decided she'd put off talking to Marcus Henry long enough. She sat at her kitchen table with the number Scott had given her and mentally reviewed the speech she'd prepared, then dialed.

"Hello?" A man answered on the second ring, his voice brusque.

"May I speak to Marcus Henry?" she asked, automatically assuming her most formal tone.

"This is Henry. Who is this?"

"Hello, Mr. Henry. My name is Marisol Luna. I'd like to talk to you about the old Palace Hotel."

"The same Marisol Luna whose picture was on the front page of the Houston paper?"

She ignored the comment. "About the Palace Hotel, Mr. Henry," she prompted.

"Are you interested in buying the place?" he asked. "A good location like that doesn't come cheap."

"I'm not interested in buying it, Mr. Henry. I understand you plan to tear down the building."

"That's right. That's a prime piece of real estate. I'm going to build loft apartments."

"Have you considered restoring the hotel for

use as offices or apartments?" she asked. "It's a beautiful building."

"It's a firetrap that's falling apart."

"The Palace Hotel has a lot of historic significance for the town of Cedar Switch," she countered. "Restoring it could greatly enhance your image in the town."

"I'm not worried about my image. Look, Ms. Luna. I'm a businessman. A smart one." Creaking noises sounded as he moved around. "Why should I spend hundreds of thousands of dollars restoring that old hotel when I can make hundreds of thousands of dollars by tearing it down?" he asked.

"That hotel is part of this town's history. Isn't that worth something?"

"Not to me. And why is it to you? You haven't lived here for twenty years—at least that's what people tell me."

She stiffened. "Have you been checking up on me?"

"Only as a potential customer. A rich, attractive widow moves to town, I'm thinking she might want to buy a home on the golf course— or a loft downtown."

"I'm not rich, Mr. Henry."

"So I learned," he said. "But you are an attractive widow. Would you like to have dinner one night? We could talk about the hotel, though I'll warn you ahead of time, you won't change my mind." His segue was as smooth as any she'd experienced, and she was momentarily taken aback.

"I don't need to have dinner with you to tell you that a group of interested citizens is looking into having the hotel declared a historic landmark," she said, recovering. "It might benefit you to work with us."

"I might be interested in working with *you*. But not on anything having to do with that old hotel."

"I'm flattered, I'm sure," she said, making a face. She knew how to cater to a powerful man's ego, if it suited her purposes. "But I'm not interested in dating anyone at the moment."

"What about Scott Redmond?"

She froze. How did he know about her and Scott? Then she realized he must be referring to the picture of them together that had appeared in the paper. "Scott is my real estate agent," she said. "The press misinterprets everything."

"Just as well. A woman like you needs to stay away from a loser like him."

"If you think he's such a loser, why did you hire him to sell real estate for you?"

Marcus laughed. "He's a good salesman,

don't get me wrong. But he's weak. You can't depend on a weak man."

She'd never been able to depend on any of the so-called strong ones either. And Scott had never struck her as weak. By overcoming his addiction, he'd proved himself far stronger than many other men she'd known.

"About the hotel," she continued. "When our request to have the property declared a historic landmark goes through, you'll be prevented by law from tearing it down."

"You think I'm worried about your group of old women?" His tone was dismissive. "The city will never go along with your so-called historical designation. Most of them think the hotel's a firetrap, and the ones who don't won't risk losing the tax dollars I've poured into the community."

"Not everything is about money."

He laughed. "You still talk like a rich woman. Only people who have money think it's not important. The truth is, this town was dying before I showed up. People don't forget that."

"What if we raised the money to buy the building from you?" she asked.

"I might sell for the right price. But I'm the only one in Cedar Switch with that kind of money."

Marisol suspected he was right, but would never let on about that to him. "I'll be in touch again, Mr. Henry," she said.

"Please do. And I'm serious about that dinner invitation."

"Goodbye," she said. She hung up the phone and sat staring at it, reviewing the conversation. She hadn't really expected Marcus Henry to change his mind about tearing down the hotel simply because she'd asked him. Today's call had been merely a courtesy, so that when she and whatever allies she could find started pushing for restoration of the hotel he couldn't say they hadn't warned him.

Scott spent the following week trying not to think about Marisol. Though he'd left her house filled with confidence about the future of their relationship, his euphoria soon faded and the nagging sensation that he was getting in over his head and risking more than he should, plagued him. Were these doubts simply anxiety getting the better of him, or common sense trying to keep him from danger?

He was sitting at his desk Wednesday morning, trying to decide whether or not to call her when his father walked in. "How's it going, son?" Jay asked, taking a seat in the client chair across from the desk.

"Good, Dad. How are you?" Scott stopped staring at the phone and focused on his father.

Jay rested his chin on his chest, deep lines etched across his forehead and on each side of his mouth. "I ran into Tiffany at the grocery store yesterday afternoon," he said.

Scott's stomach clenched, but he kept his face expressionless. "Oh?"

"She told me the two of you had split up."

"Yes. Her idea, not mine." Though he hadn't objected.

"You don't seem too upset about it."

"Tiffany's a fine woman, but I'm not sure she's the one I want to spend the rest of my life with." He focused his gaze on the printout of a subdivision plat that hung on the wall behind his father. He could feel Jay's gaze on him, scrutinizing him the way he had when Scott was a boy and Jay suspected him of lying. In the silence that stretched between them he became aware of the ticking of the clock on the wall and the low murmur of traffic on the highway two blocks away.

"Does this have anything to do with Marisol Luna?" Jay asked after a moment.

The question startled him. "Is that what Tiffany told you?"

"No. But people have seen you with her around town. I understand you spent part of Sunday at her house."

So "people" had noticed that, and felt compelled to report it to his father. As if he was a teenager caught drinking out behind the field house after the football game. He felt sick to his stomach at the thought, but why should he be surprised? A certain percentage of folks considered it their moral duty to keep an eye on anyone they'd pegged as a troublemaker, which included anyone like him, who'd made any missteps in the past. At least no one had noticed her visit to his house Friday evening.

"Marisol and I are friends." He winced inwardly at the defensive sound of the words. Yes, he and Marisol were friends, but he couldn't deny his feelings went deeper—too deep to share with his father, or with anyone else.

"Marisol is certainly an attractive woman," Jay said slowly, as if weighing each word carefully. "She's had a lot of trouble in her life."

"All the more reason to try to help her out." He clicked his mouse and woke his computer out of hibernation, a signal to his father that the conversation was ended.

The chair creaked as Jay shifted position. "I'm not saying Marisol isn't a nice woman, but not everyone sees her that way," he said. "I'd hate to see you throw away everything you've worked so hard for on a woman who doesn't even plan to stay in town."

As if he needed to be reminded that Marisol intended to leave Cedar Switch. "The day I choose my friends based on public opinion is the day I stop calling myself a man." He glared at his father. "That's not the kind of person you raised me to be."

Pain flickered in Jay's eyes, but was quickly suppressed. "I raised you to think for yourself," he said. "To make smart decisions."

A reminder of all the dumb decisions Scott had made went unsaid. So he'd made bad choices before. Marisol was not one of them. "I'll be okay," he said. "You don't have to worry." He clicked the mouse again, opening a new listing form, still hoping his dad would take the hint. If he'd been a teenager, he'd have told his father to get off his case. But he had too much respect for Jay—and was too mindful of all his father had done for him—to take that approach now.

More silence, during which Scott stared at the blank listing form and his father made no move to leave. "How have you been feeling?" Jay asked finally.

Another topic of conversation Scott didn't relish discussing. But how could he tell his father to mind his own business when not minding it had pretty much saved Scott's life before? "I'm fine," he said.

"You still taking your medication?"

"Yes." Scott spoke through clenched teeth. How many years post rehab without a relapse or meltdown would it take before his father trusted him to look after himself?

"Good." Jay stood. "I'd better get on over to the courthouse. Judge Hanstable has a fit if anyone's late."

Scott stood also. "Hanstable. That's juvenile court, isn't it?"

Jay nodded. "I'm defending a thirteen-year-old charged with arson. He was skipping school, smoking in the woods and started a brush fire. There was no serious damage, so I'm hoping to get the sentence reduced with the promise of community service and counseling."

"Good luck with that." Scott shoved his hands in his pockets. Both men were more relaxed now that the conversation had turned to more mundane topics.

"He's a good kid," Jay said.

"You say that about all of them." About half of Jay's case load was juvenile crimes. He'd never advertised himself as a juvenile specialist, but word had gotten out that he cared about kids and did a good job defending them.

"Mostly, it's true." He leaned across the desk and patted Scott on the shoulder. "Take care. Stop by for supper soon. Your mom would like that."

"I will." He watched his dad leave, a slightly rumpled figure shuffling out of the office and down the hall, whistling tunelessly under his breath. Jay wasn't a big man, but Scott wondered if he'd ever get over seeing his dad as larger than life.

Sometimes he thought it would have been easier if Jay had berated him for his screw-ups, or had admitted he was ashamed of having a son who'd been a drug addict and a thief. Instead, his father had never said a word about Scott's mistakes, only offered every kind of help possible to correct them. Though no one had ever said anything, he knew Jay had persuaded Marcus Henry to list his new development with Scott, and Jay had paid for the months-long stay in the expensive drug rehab center in Houston. Scott was grateful, but at the same time felt weighed down by his obligations to his father. How did you ever repay a man for the sacrifices he'd made not just to his bank account, but to his pride? Jay's generosity had given Scott his life back again, but Scott couldn't help but wonder if he would ever truly feel like his life was his own. People said love didn't have a price, but maybe those were people who'd never had such a large debt to pay.

Marisol's first dance class met Thursday afternoon—eight little girls aged eight to thirteen, including Jessica's daughter, Shawna. Marisol had them each introduce themselves and talk about what they'd learned from Mrs. Peabody, then she put on music and they practiced basic positions and some simple choreography.

At the end of the class the girls crowded around her, bombarding her with questions and comments. "That was so much fun." "If my friend Carly comes next week, can she join, too?" "You're prettier than our last teacher." "Will we have a recital?" "Will there be costumes?" "My brother says I dance like a giraffe. You don't think I dance like a giraffe, do you?"

When Jessica arrived to pick up Shawna, Marisol invited her to stay for coffee. "Toni and Shawna can visit while you and I talk," she said.

"Cool." Toni grabbed Shawna's hand. "Come to my room and I'll show you the cool new computer program I got."

"I'm glad the girls are getting along so well," Marisol said as she led the way into the kitchen. "I think Toni was having a hard time making friends at school."

"I wish *I'd* been a better friend to you when we were at school," Jessica said.

Marisol poured two cups from the pot she'd started brewing before class started. "There's nothing we can do about that now. But I really want things to be different for Toni. I think having Shawna for a friend helps."

"And Calvin's her friend, isn't he?"

"Yes, but I worry about her getting *too* close to a boy at her age," Marisol said.

"Is there anything we mothers *don't* worry about?"

"No, I guess not." Had Mercedes worried about Marisol? She must have. As a teenager, Marisol might have been too caught up in her own problems to notice.

"It looks like the class was a hit," Jessica said, taking a seat at the kitchen table.

Marisol nodded. "I'm excited. The girls were

wonderful and I enjoy teaching even more than I thought I would."

"They obviously adore you." Jessica grinned. "Mrs. Peabody wasn't nearly as glamorous."

Marisol looked down at her black tights and leotard and laughed. "This is not glamorous."

"You're wearing diamond earrings and the combs in your hair are straight out of last month's *Vogue*. Your manicure and makeup are perfect. Believe me, for Cedar Switch, you're pretty glamorous."

"Hmm." Marisol sipped her coffee. "According to Marcus Henry, I'm a rich widow who'd be perfect to buy one of the lofts he plans to build where the hotel is now."

"You talked to him?" Jessica's eyes widened.

"I called him to ask him to consider restoring the hotel instead of tearing it down."

"And what did he think of that idea?"

"History means nothing to him. It's all about money." She shrugged. "About what I expected."

"Damon says it would take a fortune to restore the building," Jessica said.

"Which Mr. Henry pointed out. He said he'd make a lot more by tearing it down."

"Then I don't see how you're ever going to convince him to change his mind," Jessica said.

"Would you really rather see that beautiful old building replaced by condos?" Marisol asked.

"No. But I don't understand why you're so set on this." She leaned across the table toward Marisol. "You don't even like this town—you've said so. What difference does that old hotel make to you?"

Marisol wrapped both hands around her coffee cup. "I have a lot of good memories associated with that hotel," she said.

"Are you talking about Mrs. Peabody's dance recitals?" Jessica asked.

"That…and my mother worked there."

"I thought she was Mr. Davies's maid."

"She was, before they married." Marisol made a face. "And afterward too, the way any wife back then was a maid to her family. But when I was little, when we first moved here, she was a maid in that hotel. She'd take me with her during the summer and I'd play on the stairwell or sneak into the ballrooms. I'd pretend I was a princess or a famous ballerina." She smiled, remembering. She and her mother had been close then, the two of them against the rest of the world.

"It was a beautiful place once," Jessica said. "We had our senior prom in the ballroom there. Of course, that was back when I really thought

I was a princess, and Danny was my prince."
She laughed. "And we know how well that
turned out."

"I can't be the only one who thinks the hotel
is worth saving," Marisol said.

"You're not," Jessica said. "A lot of people
have been upset about it, but no one felt they
could stand up to Henry."

"Why wouldn't they stand up to him?"

"They all have to live with the consequences.
And, he's done a lot of good things for the
town. They don't want to appear ungrateful.
Some of them are afraid if they tick him off
he'll take his money—and the jobs and pros-
perity that came with it—and leave."

"And I'm an outsider whose reputation is already shot." Marisol set down her cup with a
hard thump. "One good thing about not giving
a damn what anyone thinks of you—it gives
you the freedom to do all kinds of outrageous
things."

Jessica studied her for a moment. "I don't
believe you don't care what people think," she
said. "No one is that cold."

"It's not coldness, it's self-preservation,"
Marisol said. "I'd have never made it through
my childhood if I'd let what people said about
me get to me."

Jessica winced. "And I was one of those people." She pushed her coffee cup aside. "I'm not trying to make excuses for what I did—it was inexcusable. But I think one of the reasons we gave you such a hard time is we were trying to get some reaction out of you. You were so beautiful and aloof. We couldn't stand it. I think if you'd broken down we would have lost interest in you."

Marisol stared at her. "That's sick."

Jessica nodded. "I know. And I'm sorry. I hate that I was ever like that."

Marisol traced her finger around the rim of her coffee mug. "Once, when I was due to testify during the murder trial, my lawyer told me I needed to cry on the stand," she said. "He told me I was too calm, too self-contained. It was making the jury, and the press, see me as cold and heartless. As if I didn't care that my husband was dead or that I might be sentenced to die for killing him."

"Oh, my gosh. What did you do?"

"I was stunned. I'd been fighting so hard to keep it together, to be strong. Inside, I was terrified, but I was afraid to let that out—afraid that if I started crying, I'd never stop." She swallowed hard, remembering. "I told him I did my crying in private. He convinced me my life depended on my changing. So I did the best I could. I choked back sobs and let my eyes water. But I couldn't really weep in public. I couldn't let myself be that vulnerable."

"People admire that strength," Jessica said. "I know I do. And some of us think that if anyone can get the better of Marcus Henry, it's you."

"Thanks. I hope that's true. This town should hold on to places like the hotel." And she should be allowed to hold on to the one place associated with truly good memories of her childhood. So much had been taken from her—her home, her mother and her husband, all the good feelings she'd once had about her marriage, about her life. The least she could do was try to save that hotel, and that one bit of untarnished innocence still left inside her.

Chapter Nine

The next morning, a florist delivered two dozen roses to Marisol's door. "Aren't you the lucky one?" the deliveryman said, grinning. "Are they from one of your rich admirers in Houston or do you have a local beau?"

"I have no idea who they're from." She signed for the delivery and shut the door in the nosy man's face. Had Scott sent these? So much for her admonition that they needed to be discreet.

She carried the flowers to the table and opened the little envelope attached to the ribbon around the vase.

Are you sure you won't have dinner with
me?
Marcus Henry

She tore the card into tiny pieces and carried
it to the trash. There was a time, not so many
years ago, when such an extravagant gesture
would have impressed her. It was the kind of
gesture Lamar had made when they were dating, one that flaunted his money and reminded
her that if she hooked up with him, she'd never
want for anything again.

Except, of course, that Lamar's money was
gone now, along with the man. And she was no
longer a poor girl who was easily impressed.
She missed having money, but she was no longer willing to sell herself to get it.

The phone rang and she frowned. Was it
Henry, calling to gloat over his gift? She snatched
up the receiver, prepared to dissuade him of any
notion that she was interested in him. Instead,
she heard Scott's voice on the line. "Hello, Marisol," he said. "How are you today?"

"Better, now that you've called." She smiled,
picturing him at his desk, tie loosened, sleeves
rolled up, hair slightly rumpled.

"Mmm." The urgency in that murmur made

her heart flutter. "I've been thinking about you. When can I see you again?"

"I want to see you again," she said. "But it's hard, with my classes up and running, and Toni…"

"One day while she's in school, then. I can come to your place, or you can meet me at mine. Or we can go to a hotel, out of town."

On the surface, the idea of sneaking off for a tryst in the middle of the day seemed exciting and sexy. The reality was more tawdry. "Don't you have clients?" she asked. "And I have things I need to do. And what if something happens and Toni needs me? I can't be off in a hotel in another town."

His sigh was heavy. Exasperated? Or merely as disappointed as she was? "You're right. I just…could I come over? And talk? I can bring new comps and some open house flyers for you to look at, if you need something to explain my being there."

She smiled. "I'd like that. And bring the comps and the flyers. I should see them, anyway."

"I'm meeting a client for lunch, but I can be there about two. Though don't think it's going to be easy for me to keep my hands off of you while I'm there."

His words sent a thrill through her. Keeping her hands off Scott was going to be a challenge as well, but she was up for all kinds of new challenges these days.

Shortly before two, Scott pulled into the driveway. Dressed in a trim gray suit and blue-and-gray striped tie, carrying a briefcase, he was the picture of the young professional on his way up.

Marisol watched from the front window until he reached the porch, then she opened the door, grabbed him by the tie and pulled him inside. She covered his mouth with her own before he could speak and within seconds they were tearing at each other's clothes, backing down the hall, bumping off walls on their way to the bedroom.

"I thought we were going to keep our hands off each other," he gasped as they fell together onto the bed.

"I changed my mind."

"I like how your mind works." He rolled her onto her back and nuzzled her breast. "I like everything about you, in fact."

She glanced at the clock. One hour before Toni was due home. "You have forty-five minutes to show me how much," she said. "Then you have to go back to your well-behaved real estate agent persona."

"Forty-five minutes?" He caressed her hip. "You may overestimate my abilities."

"Oh, no. I'm quite sure you're up to the task." She stroked his erection, and his eyes took on the slightly glazed look she was growing to adore.

"Maybe the key is making you forget all about time," he said, lowering his head to her breast once more. "The way you make me forget everything when I'm with you."

That was part of the beauty of being with him, Marisol mused as he kissed his way down her body. When she was with Scott, she was able to forget the pain of the past and the uncertainty of the future. He reminded her of how wonderful it was to be with him in this moment, alive and cherished by a wonderful man.

Then all thought vanished as he gently parted her thighs and his mouth wholly claimed her. She threaded her fingers in his hair and closed her eyes, surrendering to the wonderful, soaring freedom.

An hour later, Marisol and Scott were seated at her kitchen table, fully dressed, papers spread out between them. Marisol's bed was made and all evidence of their lovemaking banished, except for the well-satisfied look in her eye, and the smile Scott could not entirely contain.

Marisol looked up as the front door opened, then slammed. *Toni* she mouthed to Scott.

"Mom!" Toni shouted.

"In the kitchen," Marisol called.

Toni stopped in the doorway and looked from her mother to Scott. Her long braids swung forward to half hide her face, but what Marisol could see was flushed and tear-streaked. "Honey, what is it?" she asked, rising from her chair.

"I don't want to talk about it with *him* here." She jerked her head at Scott.

"I can go," he said, gathering up the papers. "Let me know what day is good for the open house," he told Marisol, though his eyes when they met hers telegraphed concern.

"Thanks," she said. For understanding her need to be alone with Toni as much as for anything else.

"I'll let myself out," he said, and retreated from the kitchen.

"Why is he always hanging around here?" Toni asked, letting her backpack slide to the floor.

"Sit down and tell me what's wrong," Marisol said, ignoring the question. "Why have you been crying?"

Toni waited until the front door clicked shut and they heard Scott's car start up. "It's all your fault," she said, with a vehemence that made Marisol feel as if she'd been slapped.

She sat across from Toni, forcing herself to remain still and calm. "What's all my fault?" she asked.

"Did you really jump off the highway bridge stark naked when you were fifteen?" Toni asked.

The unexpectedness of the question, and its innocence compared to all the other things Toni might have asked, surprised a laugh from Marisol. "Is that what this is all about?" she asked.

"Then it's true?" Toni's voice rose and broke. "Mom, why? Do you know how embarrassing this is?"

"I promise you, at the time I didn't have any thought of embarrassing my future teenage daughter."

"But why would you do something like that? In front of the whole town?"

"It wasn't the whole town. Just a bunch of my classmates." She remembered Scott said he'd been there, though at the time when she'd looked down from the bridge, all she'd seen was a sea of mocking faces. "I did it on a dare."

"On a dare? Mom, how could you?"

"It was a long time ago. It doesn't matter now." She was surprised anyone still remembered. "Who told you about it?"

"One of the girls in my class brought her aunt's yearbook to school. She showed me the notes in the back where they write all the school gossip from the year. One of the notes was 'No one will ever forget when M.L. jumped off the bridge wearing only the skin God gave her. The daring Miss L always knows how to get attention!' The girl said M.L. was you!"

"It was me. And it was a foolish thing to do. I'm sorry it embarrassed you, but I can't do anything to take it back."

"You're always doing things to embarrass me," Toni wailed.

"That's not true. I've never purposely done anything that would hurt you in any way."

"Like your getting arrested wasn't the most horrible thing that could happen to me?"

"That wasn't my fault!" Marisol protested. Tears pricked her eyes and she blinked them back. Toni was hurting; she couldn't realize how much she was wounding Marisol with her words.

"Maybe not that," Toni conceded. "But what about that picture in the paper of you and Scott? If you hadn't insisted on trying to be a waitress, that wouldn't have happened. I hate it that you let him hang out here all the time."

"Scott does not *hang out here all the time*."

"Did he send you those roses I saw in the living room?"

"No, he did not."

"They're from someone else?" Toni's eyes widened. "Mom!"

"The roses are from a man who has asked me out, but I have absolutely no interest in dating him, and I've told him so."

Toni looked a little less alarmed, though her expression was still glum. "I still don't like Scott coming around here."

"What exactly do you have against Scott?" Marisol asked. "He's a nice guy."

"I don't like the way he looks at you."

"What way does he look at me?"

Toni wrinkled her nose. "All moony. Like he's in love with you or something."

"He does not!" Scott was not in love with her. He'd just broken up with one girlfriend.

He didn't want another. He knew she wasn't staying in town.

Toni watched her mother through veiled lashes. "Sometimes you look at him that way, too."

Marisol shook her head, sure she hadn't heard Toni right. "I am not in love with Scott Redmond," she said. "He's just a friend."

"How could you love anyone else after Dad?" Toni asked, ignoring Marisol's protests.

As Marisol looked at her daughter's sorrowful expression, understanding dawned. Toni's distress wasn't about Scott or Marisol being in love as much as it was about missing her father. "Toni," she began, searching for the right words. "Just now, you said my being in jail was the worst thing that ever happened to you. I would have thought the worst thing was when your father died."

"Well, yeah, it was."

"Do you want to talk about it?" Marisol's arrest had prevented them from discussing Lamar's death right after it happened, and later Marisol had been too focused on wanting to move forward with her life to revisit the past. But maybe Toni needed to talk about the subject.

Toni's eyes met Marisol's. "No. Talking just

makes it worse. Just— Don't get involved with this Scott guy. It's too soon. Maybe later, like in a few years, when I'm older, you'll meet somebody nice. But it's too soon."

Marisol flashed back to her own pain when Mercedes had decided to marry Harlan Davies. If she'd had the courage then to ask her mother to call off the engagement, would Mercedes have done so? Maybe that was pointless speculation, but it was the reminder Marisol needed that she'd never put a man above her daughter and she'd never allow an estrangement with Toni like the one she'd had with Mercedes. "All right, baby."

"I'm going to my room. I just want to be alone."

Marisol pressed her lips together to keep from calling out as Toni shuffled from the room. Though she'd never intended to do so, Marisol had caused her daughter more pain than anyone so young should have to endure.

Marisol had been selfish, thinking only of her own happiness, when she should have been considering Toni more. Her job right now was to be the best mother she could be, and to help Toni through these difficult times. She would do anything to keep her daughter from suffering more—even end her affair with Scott.

* * *

"I want to welcome you all to this first meeting of what I hope will be a group dedicated to preserving local historic structures." Marisol faced the men and women clustered around tables in the Bluebonnet Café, which Mary had agreed to open after hours for their meeting. She was grateful the tablecloth hid her shaking legs, and kept one hand on the back of her chair for support. She'd addressed groups like this before, but then she'd been Marisol Dixon, wife of a wealthy and famous man. Now she was Marisol Luna, the less affluent yet still notorious accused murderess and town bad girl.

Just then, the door opened and Scott slipped inside and took a seat at a table near the back. Marisol hadn't seen him in the two days since Toni had interrupted them, and she was surprised by how hard her heart pounded now. She hadn't told him of her decision to break off their affair, and wondered how he'd take the news. She hoped he'd understand this wasn't about him or her own feelings, but what she had to do for her daughter's well-being.

She tore her gaze from him and focused her attention once more on her purpose here. "I'm really pleased so many of you came out tonight," she said. Besides Jessica, Mary and

Scott, eleven other people had shown up—nine women and two men. They stared up at her now with expressions ranging from open suspicion to warm interest. She suspected a few of them had shown up for the chance to get a closer look at her, but she hoped to convince them to help her with this project.

She cleared her throat and soldiered on. "I've passed out brochures from the Texas Historical Commission that explain requirements for designation as a historic landmark, and the application process," she said. "As I mentioned in my invitation, I'm particularly interested in trying to have the Palace Hotel designated as a landmark."

A white-haired man raised his hand and Marisol nodded to him. "Marcus Henry owns that hotel," he said. "What does he think about this project of yours?"

"Mr. Henry wants to tear down the hotel and build loft apartments," she said, though she was sure this was news to no one in the room. "He isn't interested in the historic value of the building."

"If it's his property, I guess he has the right to do what he wants with it," her questioner continued. "What right do we have to stop him?"

She tightened her grip on the chair. "I've approached Mr. Henry about working with us, but he wasn't receptive," she said. She had, in fact, spoken with Marcus several times in the past week, though he refused to discuss the hotel. He continued to ask her out. She continued to refuse, though he laughed every time she said no.

"I'm a very persistent man," he'd told her. "I'm used to getting what I want, whether it's a building or a woman."

The words were the overly dramatic dialogue of a B-movie villain—except that, from everything she'd heard about the man, they appeared to be true. The people of Cedar Switch had given him free rein as long as he kept money flowing their way.

"What if we did succeed in getting the hotel designated as a landmark?" A large, blond woman spoke from the left side of the room. "Who's going to pay for the upkeep of the building then? A building that old probably needs all new wiring and plumbing and no telling what else."

Others murmured and nodded their heads in agreement.

"There are grants we can apply for to help defray some expenses," Marisol said. "But that's a good question. Does anyone know for sure what kind of shape the wiring and plumbing are in? Has there been any kind of inspection? I looked and couldn't find anything in the public records."

"Whatever shape it's in, it's old and it's bound to need updating," another woman said.

Had they all showed up in order to disdain the idea of saving the hotel? She glanced at Jessica, who gave her an encouraging smile. She avoided looking at Scott, afraid her face might betray too much to him. Toni's charge about their moony expressions rang too recent in Marisol's ears. She took a deep breath and tried again. "I'm here today because I believe the Palace Hotel adds a lot of grace and character to the downtown area," she said. "It could be transformed into a museum and office space without harming its integrity. But if you would really rather have a bunch of lofts in its place—"

"This town needs lofts like I need a hole in my head." A thin woman with an unruly mass of gray curls stood and faced the gathering. "Who do you think is going to live in those lofts?" she asked. "A bunch of second-home owners from the city, that's who. Don't we have enough of those out at that golf course Marcus Henry is building?"

"Now, Edie, we don't know that," the second man, a beefy fellow with a monk's tonsure of fading blond hair, said. "We don't even know what these lofts will look like. They might be even better looking than the old hotel."

Edie snorted. "Fat chance of that. They'll be some modern glass and steel structure. Marcus Henry may have a lot of money, but he didn't use any of it to buy good taste."

Marisol managed to keep back her grin. "I think the Palace Hotel is an important part of the history of this town," she said. "It seems a shame to lose that for the sake of one man's greed."

"My wedding reception was held in the hotel ballroom," a woman said.

"The Masons met there for years, in a room upstairs," the beefy blond added.

"My grandparents always stayed there when they visited," Mary said. "It was the nicest place in town back then—the first building to have air-conditioning."

Marisol allowed her smile to show now. They were starting to understand why the hotel was worth saving.

"I'm not saying this is a bad idea." A woman

in a red sweater spoke from the back of the café. "But you know there are going to be people who say you came to town intending to stir up trouble."

"You say that like it's a bad thing," Edie said before Marisol could answer. "Sometimes troublemaker is another word for a person who gets things done that nobody else has the guts to do."

"If we're really going to try to do this, how do we get started?" Jessica asked.

Marisol checked the notes she'd made the night before. "We need a written history of the building," she said. "Old photographs of the building in its prime. It would also help to have an idea of what kind of shape it's currently in, what repairs would need to be made and that sort of thing."

"We'll never get inside without Henry's permission," the gray-haired man said.

"Then we'll have to make do with what we can see without trespassing," Marisol said.

"I can ask Damon to give us his opinion," Jessica said.

"That's great."

"I'm president of the historical society, so I can help with the history," Edie said.

"I have old photographs from when my family had the photography studio on the square," another woman offered.

"Wonderful." Marisol closed her notebook. "Why don't we plan to meet again next week and see what we have? Then we can work on compiling a report and completing the application for the state."

They agreed and the meeting was adjourned. As Marisol gathered her papers, several people came up to voice their support, including Edie.

"I remember you as a girl," she said.

"You do?" Marisol eyed her warily.

"Yes. Your mother cleaned house for me and sometimes she would bring you with her. You were only about four years old at the time. A beautiful child."

"I'm sorry. I don't remember you."

"No reason you should. Even then, you were terribly independent for your age." Edie nodded. "I knew then you'd never be one to merely go along with the crowd, and I guess you've proved me right."

"I'm sure my life would have been easier if I'd been better at conforming."

Edie smiled. "Easier maybe, but probably not as interesting." She shouldered her purse. "I'll get to work on that history right away and I'll be in touch."

She stared after the older woman, intrigued by this glimpse of her younger self, then a voice behind her said, "You did a great job tonight."

She turned to Scott and tried to smile, but all the adrenaline of the evening had deserted her and she felt closer to tears. "Thanks," she said, and eased into a chair, fearful her shaking legs would give out at any minute. "It went better than I expected."

"Are you kidding?" he said. "They loved you." His eyes shone with admiration, and other emotions she didn't want to examine too closely.

"Not everyone," she said, thinking of the woman in the red sweater and the blond man.

"Yes, everyone," he insisted.

"Whether they admit it or not, they hate that Marcus Henry and his millions have had everyone under his thumb for so long," Jessica said, joining them. "They like the idea of getting the better of him."

"And they like the idea of letting me take the blame, I'm sure," Marisol said, feeling strong enough to stand now. She wasn't going into this with any illusions of being seen as noble or particularly virtuous. But she'd stopped worrying about her image months ago. Once you'd been vilified in the press for murdering your husband, very little else had the power to wound.

"This is going to be great." Jessica gathered her belongings and walked with Marisol and Scott to the door. "Marcus Henry won't know what hit him." She waved goodbye and crossed the street to her car.

"Marcus won't like this," Marisol said, turning to Scott. "Isn't he a friend of yours?"

Scott shook his head. "Not a friend. I'm not sure Marcus has any close friends, at least not in Cedar Switch."

"Still, I'm surprised you came here tonight." She started walking down the sidewalk toward the lot next to the café where she'd left the Corvette.

"I wanted to support you," he said.

"I appreciate that," she said.

He touched her arm. "Do you have to go home right away?"

His fingers were warm, his caress gentle, with an underlying strength that made her want to lean into him. But she'd relied on her own nerve and grit too long to give in so easily. "Toni's home alone," she said, pulling away.

He started to protest, she could tell, but he closed his mouth and shook his head. "You're right, your daughter needs you."

"She does. Now that she's a teenager, she may need me even more." She glanced around, making sure no one could overhear. "Scott, I really can't see you again," she said, the words coming out in a rush. "Not alone."

"Why not? Has someone said something? Do they suspect—"

"Nothing like that. It's Toni. She's upset at the idea that you and I might even *like* each other. If she knew we were sleeping together…" She shook her head. "She's still grieving terribly for her father. The idea of me being interested in another man is painful to her."

"Does she expect you to spend the rest of your life alone?"

"No. I just think that with all the upheaval in her life lately, it's too soon to impose any more change on her life." She touched his hand, unable to keep from that contact any longer. "I enjoyed every minute we spent together, and I'll never forget it. But it's time to move on. I'll only be here a little while longer, anyway, so this is for the best."

"Don't I get an opinion?" His voice was rough, his eyes stormy. "What if I don't think it's for the best?"

She withdrew her hand. "Scott, don't make this harder than it already is."

"No. I've done everything else you've asked. I've met on your terms, and been completely discreet. But I won't pretend my feelings for you are a switch that I can turn on and off."

"I'm sorry. But my daughter has to come first." She turned away, and hurried toward her car. She told herself she and Scott could still be friends, but she knew that was a lie. There was too much heat and emotion between them for that, a connection she couldn't explain that both drew her and frightened her.

She wanted to take the words back. To tell him she would continue to see him. She wanted to believe Toni would get used to the idea that her mother might want to be with someone other than Lamar.

She climbed into the car and sat, her hand on the key in the ignition, but not yet turning it. Being with Scott was so tempting, but why open Toni—and herself—up to that heartache? While Toni may have overreacted to seeing the two of them together, she had said one thing that had the ring of deep truth.

If Marisol wasn't already in love with Scott, she was very close to falling for him, and falling hard. The hurt she could be in for if that happened was beyond thinking about. Just as well she should end things now and avoid any more heartache. He was rooted here; she had no intention of staying.

She no longer believed she'd get used to being alone, but she wasn't sure she had what it took to make a successful relationship. Lasting love seemed to require a naïveté and optimism she could no longer muster. That part of her had died with Lamar's betrayal, or maybe even before that, murdered as surely as he had been, and just as unlikely to be resurrected.

Chapter Ten

The Friday edition of the *Cedar Switch Gazateer* carried a story about the inaugural meeting of Citizens to Preserve Historic Cedar Switch, with a picture of Marisol standing behind a table at the front of the café, looking every bit as defiant and beautiful as she had the day she'd jumped from the bridge, albeit this time fully clothed and twenty years older.

Scott stared at the photograph for a long time, trying to read in her expression something of what she might be feeling for him. Her announcement that she wanted to break off their affair had been a sucker punch from which he was still reeling.

They had been so good together. They'd been discreet and he'd made no demands on her. Yes, Marisol was a mother, and naturally she would think of her child first. But what had he done that Toni objected to? He had no doubt she was still grieving for her father, but how did seeing her mother happy with someone else aggravate that grief?

He'd wanted to argue against the decision, to plead his case or find a way to refute Marisol's logic. But when he'd looked in her eyes, he'd glimpsed something that made him hold his tongue. She was clearly distressed at breaking up with him, but she was relieved also— and maybe a little afraid. She wasn't afraid of him, he was sure. But she was afraid of something inside herself, some part of her he was powerless to reach.

Only that hint of fear and his uncertainty about his ability to rein in his emotions had made him turn his back and walk away from her. But things were far from over between them. Now that he'd been a part of her life, he wouldn't leave so easily.

All morning after the paper hit the streets he waited for his phone to ring, for Marcus Henry to bellow more threats or demands. That the developer was angry he had no doubt. For too many years now Henry had gotten his own way. And truthfully, until Marisol raised the issue of the hotel, no one had been too upset about anything Henry had done. The golf course and other developments he'd shepherded were seen as good things for the area by most people, bringing in much-needed tax dollars. Any objections to Henry's plans were always quickly hushed up. All that public approbation had fueled the man's natural arrogance. Now that someone—Marisol—was standing up to him, Scott was sure he'd find some way to fight back.

By midafternoon Scott was unable to sit still or focus on anything. He paced the office, trying to remember the breathing exercises he'd been taught to ward off panic. He popped another Xanax and told himself the medication would work if he gave it time.

His first panic attack had overtaken him while he was in the treatment center, withdrawing from his addiction to methamphetamines. He'd been sitting in a group therapy session, trying to listen to another patient describe his lousy childhood, when his heart had started pounding and he'd found it difficult to breathe. Paralyzing fear had washed over him. He had never been the nervous, fearful type. In fact, he'd often been described as brash. But in those moments he'd been utterly terrified, sure he was going to die.

He hadn't died, of course. Not then, or during any of the subsequent attacks, which could hit without warning. Panic Disorder was the official diagnosis, most likely caused by a chemical imbalance brought about by the drug addiction. A lasting reminder of his own reckless stupidity.

This weakness angered him, and for the first weeks after his diagnosis he'd told himself he was strong enough to beat back this particular demon on his own. After all, he'd gotten off the meth. He'd faced down the whispers and stares of everyone in his hometown. All he had to do was get a grip on himself.

But when the panic had hit at his parents' dinner table, terrifying his mother and father to within inches of real heart attacks, Scott had admitted defeat and started therapy and medication. Both had helped, though he still had to be on his guard. No matter what, he vowed he would never give in to the fear. He wouldn't let this illness change him. If anything, he pushed himself to be even stronger because of it. And that determination had him in a white knuckle battle against the anxiety that now threatened whenever thoughts of Marisol approached.

By three thirty, he'd decided he had to get out of the office. He'd drive around looking at recently listed properties and perhaps find some to show new clients. He'd avoid Marisol's neighborhood.

He was on his way out the door when the phone rang. He froze and stared at it, waiting for the answering machine to pick up, sure he'd hear Henry's angry voice.

"Hello? Scott? This is Marisol, I—" She took in a jagged breath. "Scott, something horrible has happened."

Marisol had been only a little concerned when the girls in her Friday afternoon dance class didn't show up on time. Maybe there was a traffic accident holding them back, or their school bus was delayed for some reason. And when Jessica's minivan pulled into the driveway she was sure her suspicions were correct and the other students would arrive shortly.

"Oh, Marisol, I'm so sorry," Jessica said as soon as she was inside the house, giving her friend a stricken look.

"You're only ten minutes late," Marisol said. "And the others aren't even here yet. Is there a traffic tie-up or something?"

"You mean you don't know?" Jessica looked even more upset.

"Know what?" A shiver of apprehension washed over her, but she tried to ignore it. "What's happened?" she asked. "Is something wrong?"

Jessica glanced at her daughter, who stood watching them, wide-eyed and silent. "Shawna, go play in Toni's room, okay?" she said.

Shawna glanced at Marisol, who nodded to her. "I'm sure Toni would like to see you," she said.

When the women were alone again, Jessica took Marisol's arm and led her into the kitchen. "You'd better sit down," she said. "I know I need to."

"What is it?" Marisol demanded, starting to feel scared. "Why are you acting so weird?"

Jessica waited until they were both seated at the table before she answered. "I don't think anyone else is coming to your class today," she said.

"Why not?"

"There are a bunch of picketers at the end of your street," she said.

"Picketers?" Marisol frowned. "What are they picketing?"

"You, actually."

"Me?" Marisol almost laughed, the idea was so absurd. "Why would they picket *me*?"

Jessica licked her lips nervously. "They have signs saying you're not fit to teach children… because of your criminal history."

"My criminal history? But I was acquitted. I didn't murder my husband."

Jessica looked away. "I know, but…people worry about their kids, you know? All it takes is one person suggesting their child might be in danger and they stay away."

"In danger?" Marisol felt sick to her stomach. "I would never hurt a child!"

"I know. I'm sorry. I—I don't know what to say."

"Who would do something like this?" Marisol asked. "Does someone in town really hate me that much?"

Jessica looked thoughtful. "People are curious about you," she said. "Maybe some of them are suspicious of you, but I can't see that you've been back here long enough to make someone hate you. Unless…"

"Unless what?"

"Well…the paper ran that article this morning about your move to preserve the Palace Hotel. Marcus Henry probably didn't like that much.

And other people might not like it, too. People who are worried about the economy or jobs."

"So Marcus Henry sent picketers to harass me?" Had she finally succeeded in offending him with her persistent refusals of his overtures, and this was his method of assuaging his bruised ego—by publicly humiliating her?

Jessica shrugged. "He may not have anything to do with it. But he's the kind of man who might put the idea into people's heads."

"But why attack me that way?"

"Maybe he thinks if you can't make a living you'll leave town and you won't bother him anymore."

"Of all the lowlife bullies." Marisol jumped up and began rummaging through a stack of papers on the counter beneath the phone.

"What are you doing?" Jessica asked.

"I'm going to call Marcus Henry and give him a piece of my mind." She punched in the phone number, stabbing at the buttons as if she was poking at the man himself.

But the phone went to voice mail after two rings. She hung up without leaving a message and began to pace. "I should sue him for libel," she said. "He's the kind of man who'd pay attention to a lawsuit."

"We don't know if he's really the one behind this. And I don't know that he's dumb enough to say anything that could be prosecuted in court." Jessica nibbled at her thumbnail. "Maybe you could call the police and ask them to make the picketers leave."

Marisol shook her head. She'd had enough dealings with police to last her two lifetimes. She stopped and stared at the phone for a long moment, then snatched up the receiver and began dialing again.

"Who are you calling now?" Jessica asked.

She ignored the question as Scott's answering machine picked up.

"Hello? Scott? This is Marisol, I—" She took in a jagged breath. "Scott, something horrible has happened."

"Marisol, what is it?" Scott's voice broke into her message.

"Can you come over here? To my house?"

"Of course. What's wrong?"

"There are picketers here. They've kept all my dance students away."

"Picketers? What are they picketing?"

"They're picketing me. They're saying I shouldn't be allowed to teach children." Her voice broke. "They're saying awful things."

"I'll be right there."

She hung up the phone and leaned against

the counter. She resented whatever was in her that had propelled her to call Scott. She didn't want to need his help—to need anyone's help. But Scott knew people in this town. He knew Marcus Henry, and might have insight into if—and why—the man would do this to her.

Jessica got up and went to the sink. "I'll make some coffee," she said. "And maybe something for the girls." She started rummaging in the cabinets.

Marisol said nothing, too numb to speak or move. When would the nightmare ever end? When would she stop paying for something she hadn't even done?

Less than five minutes later the doorbell rang. "I'll get it!" Toni shouted, and raced to the door, followed by Shawna.

"Toni, wait!" Marisol called, galvanized into action.

But Toni had already opened the door. Thankfully, only Scott walked in, and not the reporter Marisol had momentarily feared. He went straight to Marisol and put one arm around her. "Are you okay?" he asked.

Marisol caught Toni's eye over Scott's shoulder and took a step back from him. "I'm angry, and feeling a little blindsided," she said. "Do you think Marcus Henry orchestrated this to get back at me for opposing his plans for the hotel?"

"Maybe." Scott's expression was grim. "He's used to getting his own way."

"So everyone tells me. As if he was a spoiled two-year-old instead of a grown man."

"Hi, Scott." Jessica stood in the kitchen doorway, arms folded across her stomach. "Did you have any trouble getting past the picketers?" she asked.

"Picketers?" Toni asked. "What are you talking about?"

"I didn't have any trouble," Scott said. "They're smart enough not to block traffic. I rolled down my window to ask what this was all about and they gave me one of these." He held out a flyer.

Marisol stared at the black-and-white photos printed on the single sheet of paper and felt a wave of dizziness wash over her. Do you want a criminal teaching your children? asked bold black letters at the top of the page. Below this were two black-and-white photographs—one of Marisol the day she was arrested and charged with Lamar's murder, being led from her River Oaks home in handcuffs. A day she'd been trying hard to forget.

The second picture was of a day she'd almost

succeeded in forgetting. This picture showed a much younger Marisol, wearing jeans and a T-shirt, escorted by two police officers, her head down, tears streaking her face. Beneath it was pasted the headline that had accompanied the picture when it ran in the local paper. Sixteen-year-old charged with attempted murder of stepfather.

"Mom, is that you?"

Marisol had forgotten for a moment that Toni was in the room. She snatched the flyer from Scott and crumpled it into a ball, but not before her daughter had gotten a good look at it.

"Mom!" Toni demanded. "That *is* you! What is this all about?"

"Maybe we all need to sit down and talk," Scott said. He led Marisol and Toni into the kitchen, where they sat at the table while Jessica fussed with the coffeepot and Shawna huddled in the corner, biting her lip.

Toni shrugged out of Scott's grasp and sat on the far side of the table, glaring at him.

Marisol turned to Jessica. "Would you mind leaving us alone for a little bit?" she asked. "I'll call you later, I promise."

"If you don't, I'll call you." Jessica patted

her shoulder. "Are you going to be all right? Can I bring you anything?"

"Thanks. I'll be okay. I've been through worse." Would she ever have the kind of life where she didn't have to say things like that?

"I'll talk to you later, Marisol."

Numb, Marisol nodded. She listened to the sound of her friend's footsteps across the wood floor of the living room turned studio, and the click of the front door as it shut behind her.

As soon as they were alone, Toni spoke, her voice shaking. "What is all this about?" she asked, looking from Marisol to Scott and back again. "Why are there picketers? Why are they handing out flyers with Mom's picture? What's this about you killing your stepfather?"

"I didn't kill him," Marisol said dully. She closed her eyes, trying to think, to push past the crushing lethargy that had overwhelmed her the moment she saw that old photograph.

"Maybe I'd better go," Scott said, sliding his chair back from the table.

"No, it's okay." Maybe she was being a coward, not wanting to face her daughter alone, but she needed Scott's calm strength. And maybe, after all this time, it would be good for someone else—another adult—to know the truth.

She smoothed the crumpled flyer out on the

table and stared at the pictures again. "That's me, when I was sixteen," she said.

"That's the year you left Cedar Switch," Toni said. "Is this why?"

Marisol nodded. "Partly."

"And you didn't think it was important to tell me?" Toni's voice rose once more, on the edge of hysteria.

"I wanted to protect you," Marisol said firmly. "You had enough to deal with between your father dying and me being arrested. Your grandparents agreed we should keep as much of the trial from you as possible." Toni had stayed with Lamar's parents during the trial. The Dixons' relationship with their daughter-in-law had been prickly at times, and Marisol knew at least in the early days of the trial, they suspected she had indeed killed their son. But the older couple thought the sun rose and set on Toni and would have done anything to protect her.

"What does this have to do with Dad's murder?" Toni asked. "This happened twenty years ago. Why didn't you ever tell me?"

"Because it's an ugly story and I saw no need to tell you," she said.

Toni glared at her, eyes red with unshed tears, hurt and fear and doubt reflected in them. "You never tell me anything. You never told me about your mother. My *grandmother*. I don't know anything about her. Don't you think that matters to me? And now I find out about this? What other secrets are you keeping from me?"

Marisol glanced at Scott, whose eyes reflected sympathy. He'd probably seen the news stories when he was a boy, not to mention all that had come out at her trial. A dirt-seeking reporter for the *Houston Chronicle* had unearthed the story of the charges levied against her when she was sixteen and made them front page news, though all mention of them had been banned at her trial.

She took a deep breath, mustering courage. "I'll tell you everything now," she said. "But only if you promise not to pass judgment until you've heard it all."

Toni remained mute, her mouth set in a stubborn line. Scott was silent also, his gaze fixed on her, as if willing her some of his strength.

"I never knew my father," she began. "He died in a construction accident when I was an infant. My mother supported us by working as a maid, both privately, and at the Palace Hotel. Until she married Harlan Davies when I was eleven, Mother and I were very close." She swallowed hard, remembering those days when her mother's world had revolved around Marisol. She could do no wrong then, and was happy in spite of their poverty and struggle.

"Harlan Davies was your stepfather?" Toni asked.

"Yes. After they married, he took up all my mother's attention."

"So you tried to kill him?" Toni's voice was scornful.

"No. Don't interrupt anymore or I won't tell you the rest."

Toni pressed her lips tightly together, anger radiating like heat from her.

Marisol pressed on. The next part was hard, but she promised to be truthful, and without the truth, how would Toni—or Scott, for that matter—ever understand what drove her?

"It turned out, Harlan wasn't only interested in my mother. When I hit puberty and started to develop, he noticed and he began…bothering me."

"He molested you?" Scott's voice was hard, the muscles of his jaw white with tension.

She nodded. "Yes. For about three years. And then I decided I wasn't going to put up with it anymore. I hid a pair of scissors under my pillow and the next time he came into my room late at night I stabbed him."

"And that's when you were arrested?" Scott asked.

"Yes. My mother heard him scream and came running into my room and saw me standing there with the scissors, and Harlan lying on the floor, bleeding. She called an ambulance and the police and I was arrested."

"Didn't you tell her what happened?" Toni asked.

"Yes. But she didn't believe me. Harlan said I'd stabbed him because I was jealous and she believed him." The pain of that truth cut deep still.

"I'm sorry you had to go through that," Scott said softly.

She looked at him again, with an odd sense of déjà vu. "Your father came to see me that first night after I was arrested. He said he would defend me, and when I told him my story, he believed me." Her eyes stung as she remembered the man who had been the one adult to treat her with tenderness during the ugly ordeal. Where others looked at her with suspicion and even hate, he'd regarded her with kind eyes and a belief in her that gave her the strength to hold her head up and look at those who would judge her in the eye. A strength she'd remembered and drawn on in the days after she was arrested and charged with murdering Lamar.

"The charges were dropped after Harlan realized the truth would come out in court," she continued. "He wasn't willing to risk his reputation as a fine, upstanding citizen if my accusations became public. And my lawyer—Scott's father, Jay—wanted to spare me any further embarrassment, so he agreed to keeping the whole thing quiet."

"He never spoke about it," Scott said. "Though I remember you coming to my house once during that time. I was fourteen and too awkward to speak to you." His voice roughened. "I thought you were the bravest girl I knew."

"What happened with Grandma Mercedes?" Toni asked.

"She told me it would be better if I didn't come back home," Marisol said. "She didn't want to risk any more trouble. That was the word she used—*trouble*—as if all of this was my fault and if I just went away, it would all be fine."

"That must have been hard," Scott said.

She nodded. "I moved to Houston, to live with one of my mother's sisters," she said.

"I still can't believe you didn't tell me," Toni said. "I mean, we're living here in this town—in this *house*—where it all happened and you didn't think it was important to at least mention it? Instead, I have to find out from some protester?" She stabbed a finger at the flyer.

"I didn't see any reason for you to know about it," Marisol said. "I never dreamed it would come up again."

"Well, it did! Can't you understand how awful this makes me feel?" She stood and ran from the room.

Marisol started to go after her, but Scott put a hand on her arm. "I know it's none of my business, but I think maybe she needs time to cool off," he said.

Marisol settled back into her chair. "You're right," she said. "And she's too angry with me right now to listen to anything I have to say. It's all more proof that I'm trying to ruin her life."

"Don't most teenagers think that?" he asked. "I know I felt that way when I was her age."

"If by ruin, you mean keep them from doing things to hurt themselves or others, and preventing them from doing everything their own way, I guess they're right." She stared at the flyer, at the combination of defiance and fear on the face of the young girl in the second photograph— an expression eerily similar to that on the face of the older woman in the picture taken only last year.

"Do you have any idea who's behind this?" Scott asked.

"I was going to ask you the same question." She turned the flyer facedown. "Do you think Marcus Henry would do something like this to get back at me for interfering with his plans for the hotel? Maybe to convince me to leave town?"

"He might. Would anyone else want you to leave for some reason?"

She shook her head. "I don't know. No one ever claimed to miss me the first time I left, but other than my run-in with the press at the café, no one's been that hostile." She'd begun to think, even, that she and Toni would be able to have a semblance of a normal life here—that she might even wait until school was out for the summer before she uprooted her daughter again.

"What about the press?" Scott asked. "Could one of them have leaked this story in order to stir up something?"

Marisol frowned. "There's no telling what the tabloids will do to sell papers. I guess it's possible."

"I'll ask a few questions, see what I can find out," he offered. "Is there anything else I can do to help?"

"Yes. Find me a buyer for this house." She wouldn't stay here one week longer than she had to. "I'll drop the price, whatever it takes to sell. Toni and I need to get away from all this."

"It's not really like you to run away from a conflict," he said.

"What do you know about it?" Just because they'd been lovers for a little while didn't give him the right to judge her.

He flipped over the flyer. "You didn't run away from your stepfather," he said. "You took a pair of scissors and made him stop hurting you." He tapped the second picture. "And when you were arrested for killing Lamar Dixon, you didn't hide from the press or sit demurely behind the defense table. You stood up and told everyone you were innocent, and you didn't let the media or the lawyers or anyone else cow you." His eyes met hers again, steel-gray and so intense. "It's one of the things I admire most about you."

Staring into his eyes this way made her heart pound and her mouth go dry. He talked about her strength, yet when she was near him she felt all her resolve weakening. She forced her gaze away from his, and straightened her shoulders. "I have to think about Toni," she said. "Staying here—exposing her to all this, this ugliness—

is hurting her. We need to move away and start fresh."

He opened his mouth, as if to protest, then closed it again and sat back in his chair. "All right. I'll increase advertising the place, maybe plan an open house. And I'll take another look at how we have it priced."

"Thank you." She stood and he rose also. "Thank you for coming over," she said. "I probably shouldn't have bothered you, but…" She shook her head. "I felt like I needed someone else here with me."

"You know you can call me anytime."

She walked him to the door, where they stood awkwardly facing each other. Any other friend, she might have offered a hug, but with Scott a touch could so easily lead to a kiss, and a kiss to so much more. As it was, the air between them was heavy with all their expectations of what might have been. She settled in the end for merely telling him goodbye, then stepped back, her arms crossed firmly over her chest, to keep herself from reaching for what she couldn't have.

Chapter Eleven

Unlike his father, who had devoted his life to helping young people and the other troubled clients who turned to him, Scott did not see himself as anyone's savior. He'd led a comfortable life that had been devoted primarily to pleasing himself. Looking back, he could see how this selfishness had led to his downfall, but even since then, he'd been too focused on his recovery to give much thought to anyone else.

Until Marisol. She was a strong woman who'd been through hell on her own and was perhaps the least likely person to need the help he felt compelled to give. He wanted to ease her burden, to take away her suffering, to see her *happy.* To do so he would risk anything—even his own happiness.

Thus, Monday morning found him waiting at Marcus's office when the developer arrived. "I hope you're here to tell me you've sold a few more golf course lots," Marcus said as he unlocked the door to his private sanctum and ushered Scott inside.

"I'm here to tell you to leave Marisol alone," Scott said.

Marcus set his briefcase on the corner of his desk. "You want to be careful around that woman," he said. "She obviously has a penchant for violence."

"I know you set those picketers on her," Scott said. "That was low, even for you."

"Good to know you have such a high opinion of me." He pressed the intercom button. "Shelly, would you bring us some coffee, please." He turned to Scott once more. "About those lots—I understand you had a couple of showings yesterday."

"I didn't come here to talk about real estate." He'd steeled himself for Marcus's anger; this studied indifference was much more infuriating.

"You're my real estate agent," Marcus said. "As far as I'm concerned, that's all we have to talk about."

"Leave Marisol alone," Scott said again.

"Or what?" Marcus sat behind his desk, his expression serene, except for the dark annoyance in his eyes.

"Or you'll have to answer to me." He didn't consider himself above violence on Marisol's behalf, though Marcus might respond better to the threat of legal action; Scott knew a good lawyer.

"Don't make idle threats." Marcus made a dismissive gesture.

The door opened and his secretary entered with a tray filled with coffee cups, sugar and creamer. When she had departed once more, Marcus continued the conversation. "No one in this town takes you seriously, so why should I?" He stirred sugar into his cup. "You're nothing but a drug addict who by all rights should be in jail right now. I gave you a chance as a favor to your father, so don't threaten me."

Marcus wielded the words like blows; Scott felt every one of them. Yet he remained calm enough to recognize this verbal bullying for what it was. "I know a few things about you," he said calmly. "And one of them is you're not dumb. You don't do any favors unless you see the benefit for yourself. You recognized I'm the best real estate agent in the county. If you didn't believe that, you never would have wasted your time with me."

One raised eyebrow was Marcus's only display of emotion at this response. "Tell your girlfriend to stop wasting her time interfering with my plans for the hotel," he said. "I've got the county on my side in this."

"If you think she's wasting her time, why are you even bothering to harass her?" Scott asked.

"I wanted to make a point about who it is who calls the shots." He sipped his coffee and regarded Scott over the rim of the cup. "It isn't her and her little citizens' group. It isn't you, either."

Scott wasn't naive enough to deny the truth in Marcus's point of view. Money and influence counted for a lot in the courts, in the media and in local commerce. Any day of the week, Marcus would win four battles out of five the sake of his reputation alone.

But that fifth battle had him worried; the picketers proved it. For too long no one had bothered to stand up to him. It had taken an outsider like Marisol, someone who didn't know Marcus's history, to defy him.

And now Scott was defying him too. Part of Marcus had to be wondering if this was a sign of things to come. "People don't like bullies," Scott said. "Even rich ones. If public opinion turns against you, the county commissioners and planning board members and others who've sided with you so far will have to listen. Marisol has friends here. Targeting her could go against you."

"Friends like you?" Marcus set aside his coffee cup, opened his briefcase and took out a stack of folders. "She was married to a wealthy, famous, handsome man. She's used to wearing diamonds and eating caviar. You don't have anything to offer her."

A red haze of anger blurred Scott's vision, and he sucked in a deep breath, trying to control his temper. Breaking Marcus's nose would feel pretty good right now. He'd feel great right up until the deputies hauled him away and charged him with assault. Marcus would love it. He'd tell everyone who'd listen how he'd been attacked in his own office by an out-of-control real estate agent, a man he'd tried to help. It just proved how unstable some people were.

Scott backed toward the door, his gaze never leaving Marcus's face. Hitting the man would be so easy, but maybe sometimes real bravery came in knowing when to walk away.

He drove back to his office, strangely elated

despite the inconclusive outcome of the meeting. Marcus might fire him. Or he might continue to ignore him, sending the message that Scott wasn't worth his notice. He probably didn't see Scott or Marisol as a real threat, but Scott had made him think about the possibility, and he counted that as a victory of sorts.

Most important of all, Scott had overcome his own inertia to *do something* on Marisol's behalf. Without the crutch of drugs he'd had a hard time finding enough bravado to get out of bed some days, yet today he'd stood up to one of the most powerful men in town and held his own. He felt more like his old, brash self than he had in over a year.

Whistling to himself, he entered his office and booted up his computer, thinking he might write a few ads for new properties. Time to get more aggressive with his sales pitches in light of the sluggish market.

While he waited for the computer, he opened the bottom drawer of the desk and pulled out a portfolio of ads from his early days at that other firm across town. On the first page his own smiling, younger self looked out at him. *Scott Redmond Knows Real Estate* proclaimed the bold headline on the ad.

Scott stared at the photo as if studying a

stranger. Had he really been that naive, idealistic young man?

The back of his neck began to tingle and his mouth went dry. Before he had time to register what was happening, his heart began to pound hard, as if it might burst through his chest. He struggled to breathe, fighting unreasonable terror. The walls of the room seemed to be closing in around him, and he gripped the edge of the desk, trying to control the shaking in his hands.

It didn't matter how often he endured these attacks, the emotions were always the same— the certainty he would die, or else go insane. The crushing weight of the fear made him sink in his chair, staring straight ahead, knowing that if he closed his eyes the sense of disorientation would be too great to bear.

Every breath was a struggle, every movement excruciating. All he could do was hold on and endure. After minutes that seemed like hours the fear began to recede, replaced by a sense of detachment, as if he was no longer in his body, but hovering somewhere over it, a dispassionate observer.

When he felt safe in moving once more, he groped in the center drawer of the desk until he found the bottle of Xanax. He swallowed two of the pills dry and sat back, waiting for the semblance of calm they provided. All the elation and happiness he'd felt earlier had deserted him, replaced by a sense of despair. Who was he kidding, thinking he was in control of his life? He'd confronted Marcus Henry as if he was some avenging knight, but what made him think Marisol needed defending? If she could have seen him five minutes ago, reduced to a shaking, panic-stricken excuse for a man, she'd have known *he* was the one who needed a caretaker.

He'd only had one panic attack in front of Tiffany. She'd panicked herself at first, but soon calmed down and taken charge with the same efficiency with which she dealt with nosebleeds, stomach viruses and preadolescent meltdowns in her classroom, administering cold compresses and sympathy, letting him know he could rely on her to be there for him.

He told himself he should have found her competence comforting, but having his lover treat him like a fourth grader hadn't put him at ease. He wasn't so macho he couldn't deal with being vulnerable in front of a woman, but with Tiffany the balance always swung too far. After that one attack he couldn't shake the sense that she was watching him for imminent signs of another breakdown, and another chance for her to pick up the pieces of his shattered self once more, ready to receive his gratitude. He didn't want to owe any man or woman that kind of debt. He didn't want the woman in his life to be so soothing; another kind of tranquilizer that didn't come out of a bottle.

Which left the question of how Marisol might respond to seeing him come apart at the seams before her eyes. She didn't strike him as the type to smother him with tea and sympathy. Then again, she was a woman with plenty of problems of her own. He wouldn't blame her if she decided she didn't need to take on his, as well. The woman who had bared her body on the Brazos River Bridge and her soul in front of a courtroom full of onlookers might decide to easiest way to deal with a man like Scott was to simply turn and walk away.

The picketers left after two days, and Marisol's spirits improved, though Toni remained sullen. Marisol let it be known she was open to talking more, but didn't press the issue. Toni was at an age where she had to work some things out for herself.

Marisol still hoped the house would sell

quickly and she and Toni could move away from Cedar Switch and start over. Away from this house and this town and all the memories, maybe mother and daughter would be less at odds with each other.

Meanwhile, she was determined to show Marcus Henry or whoever had targeted her that she was not afraid. So she sent a notice to her students that dance class would continue and she welcomed any who wanted to attend.

A couple of students did withdraw, but most chose to return. "I got one of those flyers, and was worried at first," admitted one young mother when she dropped off her daughter for a beginning ballet class. "But I talked to a few people and I found out *why* you attacked that man and well, I only hope in the same situation I'd have been as brave."

Marisol listened to this explanation, too astonished to respond with more than a brief, "Thank you."

"We women need to support each other," another mother said, while a third said she didn't have any use for people who tried to make trouble for other people who weren't doing anything wrong.

"Did you say anything to people about what happened with my stepfather?" Marisol asked

Jessica when the two women had a moment alone. She had telephoned her friend after her talk with Scott and told her everything that had happened during that horrible time twenty years ago.

Jessica's fair complexion flushed. "I might have mentioned it to few people," she said. "I didn't like people thinking you were some cold-blooded murderess. Besides," she added, "people in this town like to gossip so much, I figured for once you should use that to your advantage."

"Thanks," Marisol said.

"I wasn't the only one," Jessica said. "I'm pretty sure Scott and his father set a few people straight on your behalf."

It was Marisol's turn to flush. The idea of Scott as her champion pleased her more than she cared to admit.

Along with keeping her dance classes going, she decided to work even harder to have the hotel approved as a historic property. She started by phoning Edie Graves, the elderly woman who headed up the historical society. "I've been compiling everything we have on the hotel's history and trying to put it into a written essay to submit to the historical commission," Edie said, speaking with the precise diction of the schoolteacher Marisol learned she had been. "It was designed by J. Riley Gordon, the man responsible for the courthouse in Waxahachie and a number of other historic buildings around the state. When it was erected in 1896, it was said to be 'comparable to the finest establishments in Houston and the most opulent hostelry in the southern portion of the Lone Star State.' That's according to a newspaper article of the time."

"That's wonderful," Marisol said. "That's exactly the kind of information we need for our application to the state."

"I'm glad you took this on," Edie said. "It's good to see young people take an interest in the past. You should join our historical society."

"Thank you, but I won't be staying in town much longer."

"Why not? Where will you go?"

"I'm not sure." She had no real ties to anywhere.

"You should consider staying here," Edie said. "We're not an isolated, backward town anymore. You could become involved, make friends. And I hear your dance classes are very popular."

Maybe I want to move somewhere where people aren't examining my life with a micro-

scope every day, Marisol thought. But despite her discomfort with the town's scrutiny, part of her was pleased to think that people cared enough to comment on the good things about her as well as the bad.

"That's good to hear," she said. "Thank you for gathering the information about the hotel's history. I'll be in touch about the application." Once Edie had written the history, they'd need to package it together with historical photos and a report on the building's current condition. There was a questionnaire and an application to complete, and filing fees to pay. Ordinarily, the process could take months, but Marisol hoped to find a way to expedite things.

Tuesday afternoon, Scott called to let her know he was bringing a couple to look at the house. It was the first she'd heard from him since she'd summoned him on Friday. She should have been pleased he was respecting her wishes and giving her space, but deep inside herself, she could admit she missed him.

Though she was anxious to sell the property, she had no interest in seeing the potential buyers. She left the house just as they were pulling up, and debated heading to the grocery store. But when she spotted the sign for the Second Baptist Church adjacent to the shopping center, she turned down the side street and parked at the gates of the cemetery next to the church.

She sat in the car for a few minutes, studying the lacy pattern of the old wrought-iron gates, Cedar Switch Cemetery scrolled across the two halves in ornate, old-fashioned script. When she was very little, attending the Second Baptist Church, the parklike stretch of land on the other side of the fence, with its shade trees, benches and rosebushes, was a fascinating place, all the more so because her mother forbade her to enter it.

When she was a teenager, her classmates would test their bravado by sneaking out here at night to drink beer or make out amongst the graves, the girls screaming or giggling hysterically at every movement in the underbrush or scrape of a tree branch against a mausoleum roof, while the boys spoke too loud in shaky voices, pretending to be brave.

After a moment, she got out of the car, and found the side gate unlocked and slipped through. The grass was thick as a putting green, damp from a recent rain. She picked her way past neatly segregated family plots and isolated headstones and monuments. The older ones were worn and streaked with moss, the surface of the markers pitted from exposure to weather.

A concrete angel with folded wings bowed its head over the grave of a child, while a white marble obelisk marked the final resting place of a town father.

Some of the stones bore elaborate inscriptions: *Here lies a beloved mother and wife, remembered in death as in life for her calm repose.*

Elgin Spenser—A Man Who Made His Mark, though what that mark might be, Marisol had no clue.

Most of the newer granite or bronze markers revealed little more than a name and the dates of death and birth.

She found what she was looking for in the far corner of the cemetery, in a plot outlined with whitewashed stone, a single slab of red-veined marble marking two graves. Harlan Ellis Davies, 1949–2001. And beside him, the dirt still bare of grass and faintly mounded, Mercedes Luna Davies, 1953–2007.

Marisol stared at the letters and numbers, waiting to feel something. She'd put off coming here, afraid of being ambushed by sadness or anger or the pain of betrayal. But as she stood beside her mother's grave, she experienced a warmth and closeness she hadn't felt in years. All she had been through in the past year, and especially everything that had happened since she'd returned to Cedar Switch, had given Marisol new insight into her mother and the life she'd lived.

Listening to Toni beg her not to make Scott part of their lives, Marisol had seen herself when she was only a few years younger than Toni. She had watched her mother allow Harlan to come between them and not known how to stop it.

But as much as Marisol sympathized with Toni and with her own younger self, the years had given her insight into her mother's feelings, as well. With a heavy heart, she realized that Mercedes might have married Harlan in order to give her daughter a better life. She had made choices not that different from the ones Marisol had made, surrendering independence for money.

Even in the end, when she'd sent Marisol away, Mercedes might have thought she was protecting her daughter. Protecting her from further assaults, while clinging to the money that paid for Marisol's education and good clothes and even the car she drove.

Like Marisol, Mercedes had no doubt thought she was being wise to put her daughter first. Yet the results had been disastrous. How much better they all would have been if Mercedes had relied on her own strength and will, rather than designing her life around a daughter who had appreciated her efforts too late.

Marisol began to cry, silent sobs shaking her shoulders, tears streaming down her face to wet her T-shirt and the ends of her hair. "I'm sorry, Mama," she whispered. "All these years, I was so caught up in my own pain, I never thought about yours."

In leaving her the house and everything else she had, maybe Mercedes had been telling Marisol she was already forgiven. That she'd never stopped loving her daughter, despite the distance between them.

By marrying Harlan, Mercedes had given her daughter many privileges and possessions. But the greatest gift Marisol had received from her mother had not been bought with any of Harlan's money. The greatest gift had been the love and devotion of those early years, when Marisol had learned what it was to be a strong woman, standing on her own. Marisol might have strayed from that ideal at times over the years, but that strength had always been within her, and it was with her now, guiding her as she struggled to make the right decisions for her life. Better decisions than the ones Mercedes had made. Better decisions than Marisol herself had made before.

* * *

After Scott dropped off the clients at his office, he returned to Marisol's house, and was waiting there for her when she returned. He'd given the two of them these past few days to cool off, to put some needed physical and emotional distance between them. He'd hoped the time apart would help him clear his head and come to some solid conclusion about his feelings for her. He'd hoped, even, that he'd be able to approach her again simply as a friend. It was what she wanted, and he ought to be able to give her that much, however differently he might feel.

"Well?" she asked as she climbed the steps toward where he stood on the front stoop.

He knew, of course, that she was asking about the couple who had toured the house. He shook his head. "They're looking for something larger. Something newer. But not everyone feels that way," he hastened to add. "We'll find the right buyer eventually."

She nodded, and leaned back against the porch post, facing him. Dressed in faded jeans and a scoop-necked T-shirt, her hair pulled back at the nape of her neck, she looked scarcely ten years older than her daughter—not so very far removed from the girl on the bridge who'd lived in his memory all these years.

So much for his vow to keep things casual. He was aware of an underlying heat between them, an unspoken attraction he found impossible to ignore. Surely she felt it, too. "Is there anything else I can help you with?" he asked.

"Maybe." She studied the toes of her tennis shoes. "I need to know more about the condition of the hotel, what repairs it might need."

"We can do some research at the courthouse," he said. "Look through building permits. That will show any major work."

She checked her watch. "I still have two hours before Toni gets home from school," she said.

"No dance classes today?"

She shook her head. "Only Wednesday and Friday afternoons right now."

"Then let's go. Your car or mine?"

"Mine." She fished the keys from her pocket and pushed them into his hand. "You drive."

He slid into the leather driver's seat and pushed it back to accommodate his longer legs. The smooth upholstery conformed to his shape and the steering wheel was a perfect fit in his hand. The assertive throb of the engine made his heart race, but not from fear. He couldn't stop grinning. "You realize this is every man's fantasy," he said as they sped along Main Street toward the courthouse.

"Researching building permits?"

"No. Driving a hot car with a beautiful woman by his side." He was tempted to keep driving, out of town, to someplace far away from their current problems. They'd spend the weekend at the beach, wading in the surf and making love in a darkened hotel room. Alone with her for a length of time, maybe he could convince her of the depth of his feelings for her—a depth even he hadn't dared plumb.

"Want to buy the car?" she asked. "I'm thinking of selling it."

"Why would you do that?"

"It's too conspicuous. And the money would come in handy."

"If you're serious, I might know some people who'd be interested, but I couldn't afford something like this."

"We can talk about it later."

When they reached the courthouse, he led the way to the basement archives, waving to the clerk as he headed for the shelves housing the building permits. "I thought everything would be on computers," Marisol said.

"Some of it is," he said, taking down a six-inch-thick binder that bristled with pink-and-yellow sheets of paper. "But we're a decade or so behind the big cities when it comes to things like that." He opened the book on a table. "Besides, there's something to be said for an actual piece of paper you can touch."

For the next hour and a half, they worked side by side, poring over the thick binders. They located permits to upgrade the wiring, one to install new elevators, and made copies of them. "There's probably other work that didn't require a permit," he said.

She sat back and stared at the scant pile of photocopies in front of them. "If we could only get inside and see what kind of shape the place is really in," she said.

"Maybe we can."

She frowned. "Do you mean break in?"

"Not necessarily. If I call the agent who has the listing and convince him I have someone who's interested in the building, I can get the code to the lockbox."

"I thought Marcus was planning on tearing the building down?"

"He is. But he'd never turn down a buyer with enough cash. That's why the For Sale sign is still there after all this time."

She still looked doubtful. "Is getting the lockbox code that way even legal?" she asked.

"You are interested in the building, aren't you?" he asked.

She nodded. "All right. Let's do it."

He checked his watch. "It's almost time for Toni to be home, and I'll have to get in touch with the listing agent. We should probably do it at a time when the chances are fewer that someone will see us and report back to Marcus. Could you get free tomorrow evening, say, about eight o'clock? Downtown pretty much rolls up the sidewalks by then."

She hesitated. "Toni will wonder where I'm going."

"Tell her you have a meeting concerning the hotel. It won't be a lie."

"All right. She should be okay by herself for an hour or two."

"Then why don't you plan to meet me at my office tomorrow evening and we can walk over to the hotel from there. It's only a couple of blocks."

At her house, he reluctantly surrendered the Corvette again and returned to his own car. Toni arrived and she and Marisol went into the house after brief goodbyes to him. He watched them go, feeling the same dissatisfaction and restlessness he always felt in parting from Marisol. Every goodbye reminded him he was closer to their final leave-taking.

He shook his head and started the car. No sense looking too far ahead. He'd see her again tomorrow night, so for now he'd focus on that.

Chapter Twelve

The next evening, Marisol left Toni doing homework and drove to Scott's office. Toni didn't ask where her mother was going, and only shrugged in acknowledgment when Marisol gave her usual spiel about not opening the door to anyone and calling Marisol right away if she needed anything. Marisol felt a little guilty about deceiving her daughter, then reminded herself that part of being a parent was revealing information only on a need-to-know basis. Toni didn't have to know every personal detail about her mother's life; she was a child, not a roommate or best friend.

Jay Redmond was just coming out of his office next door to Scott's when Marisol arrived, and he frowned at her. "Hello, Marisol," he said, subtly checking her out—not in the way a man checks out a woman he finds physically attractive, but in the way he might scrutinize a guilty suspect on the stand in court. She had dressed carefully in black jeans, boots and a sleeveless black sweater, an outfit appropriate for skulking about in the shadows. "I wondered why Scott was staying at the office so late," Jay said.

"Marisol and I have some business to attend to." Scott emerged from his office. He, too, was dressed in black, a color that made him look slightly dangerous and sexier than ever.

Jay continued to frown. "Where are you going?" he asked.

"Out." Scott turned to Marisol. "Are you ready?"

She nodded, avoiding Jay's steady gaze. The older man turned away from them at last and walked to his car. "See you tomorrow," he called over his shoulder. "Good night, Marisol."

"Good night, Jay." The words were swallowed up in the roar of the engine as he started his car and drove away.

"Your dad doesn't look too happy about

seeing us together," she said as she and Scott started walking toward the hotel.

"He worries too much," Scott said.

"What does he have to worry about?"

He shoved his hands in his pockets and stared straight ahead. "He worries I'm getting in over my head with you. That you have too many problems and I can barely handle my own."

A chill swept over her. "What kind of problems do you have?"

He pulled one hand from his pocket and held it out. In it was a pill bottle. She hesitated, then took it.

"Xanax?" She read the label. "That's for anxiety, right?"

"Right. Have you taken it?"

She nodded. "My doctor prescribed it for me during the trial. It helped, some."

He pocketed the bottle again. "There are days I can't get through without it."

She stared at him, not knowing what to say. Scott always seemed so confident and energetic—so happy. Was she mistaking nervousness for energy and bravado for confidence? Or was it only that she sensed the strength that allowed him to persevere despite his challenges?

They reached the hotel and climbed the steps leading to the wide front veranda in silence. Scott opened the lockbox and retrieved the key and they stepped inside. "Wait a minute, I've got a flashlight," he said. A moment later the thin beam of a pen light played across the faded maroon carpet of the lobby. Marisol followed the path of the light across the carpet and up the front desk. Dust coated the brass-trimmed wood of the check-in desk, and cobwebs festooned the row of cubbies on the wall behind the counter. A notice tacked on a bulletin board next to the cubbies advertised the annual awards dinner for the Rotary Club to be held in the hotel's main dining room.

Scott moved the light upward, until the beam focused on the chandelier over their head. Tiers of crystals reflected the light and pointed down at them like teeth in the mouth of a shark.

"Let's check out the dining room," Scott said.

She followed him across the lobby, to the double frosted glass doors that led to the Palace Arms restaurant. The doors were stiff, and Scott had to pull back hard to open one. Marisol moved past him and stood in the foyer by the reservation desk, staring at a scene out of a dream.

Rows of tables stood ready, draped with faded pink damask cloths, flowers withered in bud vases at the center of each one, gilt-trimmed chairs drawn up to them, in pairs or four or six or eight to a table. At one end of the room the steam table and salad bar sat silent and empty, as if awaiting the arrival of the day's offerings. Banks of green palm trees stood alongside windows over which hung heavy pink and gold drapes. Marisol walked over and ran her hand along one of the palm fronds. Her fingers came away coated with dust, the silk of the artificial plant trembling in the aftermath of her touch.

"I can't believe the owners walked off and left everything like this," she said.

"I believe they'd been losing money on the place for a while," Scott said. "They were probably glad to accept Marcus's offer."

They left the dining room and returned to the lobby, walked past telephone kiosks complete with old-fashioned heavy black pay phones, past the ornately etched brass doors of the elevators to a sweeping marble staircase that led to the second floor.

Marisol climbed the steps behind Scott, trailing her hand along the smooth walnut railing, remembering the time she'd slid down this same railing, landing in a heap at the bottom. She'd surprised the desk clerk and earned a spanking from her mother, who had reminded her that she was to be invisible while Mercedes worked, and that her failure to do so could cost Mercedes her job.

On the second floor, Scott opened a door to reveal a meeting room, empty except for a broken easel and a brass plaque that proclaimed this was where the Lions Club met the third Thursday of each month. Other doors revealed similar rooms.

On the third floor, they entered the first of the guest rooms. Two double beds draped in polyester bedspreads in muted shades of maroon and green shared space with a green-upholstered side chair, a Queen Anne style desk and chair and a built-in dresser. Marisol pulled back the matching green and maroon drapes and the glow of a streetlight outside revealed only a light coating of dust. A single towel, a roll of toilet paper and two glasses furnished the bathroom.

"The plumbing seems to work," he said, turning the taps on and off and lifting the lid to check the toilet. "The place could use paint and some new carpet, but the floors feel sound enough underfoot."

She returned to the bedroom and sat on the side of the bed. Scott turned from his inspection of the closet and saw her. "Are you okay?" he asked.

"I was remembering when I was a little girl and would come here with my mother," she said. "I would sit in the chair and read or color or watch television while she worked. When she wasn't running the vacuum cleaner, we'd talk."

"What did you talk about?" he asked.

"Everything. The story I was reading or people on TV. Sometimes we talked about what it would be like to have as much money as the people who'd rented the room. We'd travel and have a lot of fancy clothes. Mostly, we just enjoyed being together." She smoothed her hand across the bedspread, the memory of those days so real she could almost smell the scent of bleached towels and lemony furniture polish. "I missed that closeness after she married Harlan." Though she thought she understood now why her mother had made the choices she had, that only lessened the pain a little.

Scott sat beside her on the bed and pulled her close. She closed her eyes, grateful she could lean on him for a while. Despite all her assertions that she wanted independence, all the bad times in her life had been made worse by having to bear them all alone. When she'd been arrested for stabbing her stepfather, and those first few years in Houston, and again when Lamar had died and during the whole awful year after that she'd had only her own strength to draw on. She'd told herself all those experiences had made her stronger, but she welcomed the opportunity to put aside her burdens briefly.

Gradually she became aware of the scent of his cologne and the rhythm of his breathing… of the man beside her who was more than a casual acquaintance and less than a lover. She raised her head and looked at him. "Tell me why you take the Xanax," she said. "What are you anxious about?"

He took his arm from around her, but did not draw away farther. Resting his elbows on his knees, he stared down at the carpet. "After I graduated college I came back to Cedar Switch," he said. "I'd made friends with a guy who was opening a real estate agency and he asked me to join him. Houston had just come out of the business bust of the '80s and people had money again. They were spending a lot of it on real estate in places like this.

"I discovered I had a talent for the business. I

liked people and I was a good salesman. I made a lot of money, more money than I knew what to do with. I was young, single and rich, and determined to have as much fun as I could." He laced his fingers together and rested his chin on his knotted hands. "I went to a lot of parties, dated a lot of women, met a lot of high rollers who were happy to help me spend my money and show me a good time. One of them introduced me to meth."

"Methamphetamines?" she asked, stunned.

"Yeah. Crystal. Crank. Amp. Tweak. Whatever you call it, I loved the stuff. I loved the energy it gave me—the way it made me feel I could accomplish anything. When I was on meth, I had no limits. I could go all night and all the next day and I felt great. I never wanted to let go of that feeling."

She heard the longing in his voice as he spoke, like a man speaking fondly of a lover he missed. "I found out after he died that Lamar was taking drugs," she said. "Cocaine and pills. It's where a lot of our money went."

He nodded. "It's an expensive habit. I couldn't keep up with the cost, so I started helping myself to money from the company accounts. I told myself I'd pay it back with my next commission, but when the next commission check came in, I needed it for drugs and credit card bills and all the other expenses of life in the fast lane. No telling where I'd be now if I hadn't gotten caught."

"What happened?"

"The senior partner called me into his office. I remember the first thing that clued me in to the fact that this wouldn't be an ordinary conversation was that my dad was there. He was a friend of the partner's. And there, in front of my father, the partner told me what he'd found, that he knew about all the money I'd stolen and why."

He hung his head. "If he'd confronted me by myself, I might have tried to bluff my way out of it, but with my dad there, all I felt was shame. He looked at me and I saw how much I'd let him down."

She put her hand on his wrist. "Your father loves you very much," she said. "Anyone who sees you together knows that."

"Oh, yeah, he loves me. He loves me enough that he agreed to pay back all the money I'd stolen. It must have about wiped out his savings, though he never said a word, and when I asked about it, he wouldn't answer. The partner agreed to accept my resignation and not file charges. My dad put me in his car and drove me straight to a treatment center in Houston. I didn't even protest. I was just…too numb."

"And the center cured you of your addiction?"

"More or less. I still crave that euphoria that I first got from the meth," he said. "But all I have to do is think of my father standing there, looking so sad and ashamed, and that feeling goes away. I spent three months in the treatment center and came home with pretty much nothing—no money, no job, my reputation in tatters. I wanted to move away, but I didn't have anywhere to go or the means to get there."

He straightened and smoothed his palms down his thighs, his voice brisker. "So I moved into my old room at my folks', turned space in my dad's office into my own real estate company, and started putting my life back together."

"That took a lot of courage," she said. "Coming back here where so many people must have known what happened."

He nodded. "They knew. It took a long time before I got my first client. But I kept my nose clean, did all the right things, and frankly, my dad helped. People in this town think a lot of him and they were willing to give me the benefit of the doubt for his sake. And gradually, I've been able to pull things together. I moved into my own place and started feeling like maybe everything would be all right."

"But what about the Xanax?"

"Oh, yeah." He sighed. "The treatment center managed to help me get off the meth, but I guess you can't screw up your body like that for months at a time and not have it come back to haunt you. The thing that stayed with me they call panic disorder. Basically, my brain chemistry gets out of whack and without warning I can have a meltdown. Complete and total panic for no reason."

"That must be terrifying."

"Exactly."

"And the Xanax keeps it under control?" Maybe that explained his seeming calm now.

"Mostly. Stress makes it worse, which is why my dad worries."

"And I'm stressful to you."

"No. When I'm with you I don't feel stressed." His eyes met hers. "I feel…strong. As if I'm exactly where I want to be."

Simple words that touched her soul. "Yes," she whispered. "I know what you mean." She leaned toward him, all the feelings she'd fought against every time she was with him overwhelming her in the wake of his laying his soul bare to her. "Right now, this is exactly where I want to be," she said. "With you."

She closed her eyes as their lips met, shutting out the faded room and the memories of the life she'd once lived here. She wanted only to be in this moment, with this man, who asked nothing of her but that she be herself, problems and complications and all.

His mouth brushed softly against hers, then more firmly, as his knuckles traced a path along her cheek. He kissed her closed eyelids, and the soft flesh beneath her ear. "I want to make love to you, Marisol Luna," he whispered.

"Yes," she said, and wrapped her arms around him and pulled him down onto the bed beside her.

The desperation of their earlier couplings was gone, replaced by a focused intensity. They undressed each other slowly, helping each other out of their clothes. With hands and mouths and eyes, they explored each other's bodies, as if determined to learn everything there was to know. Beneath this scrutiny, Marisol felt more naked than she ever had, yet freer too. With Scott, she felt no need for pretense. She wanted nothing more from him but his presence in this moment.

They lay facing each other on the bed, stroking and kissing, letting the heat between them build. The sweetness of the moment was spoiled only by Marisol's innate caution. "You remember I told you I'm not on any kind of birth control," she said.

"Not to worry." Scott rolled over and retrieved his pants from the floor. In a moment, he faced her once more, brandishing a condom packet like a trophy.

"I don't know whether to be impressed or horrified," she said. "Or do you always carry condoms, as a matter of course?"

"Only since I've been seeing you."

"You were that confident you'd get me back in bed?"

"I told you I knew what I wanted," he said.

"Seems like you were pretty sure you'd get it." The same words that had offended her when spoken by Marcus Henry made her feel both cherished and powerful now.

"The heat the two of us have been generating when we're together, I figured it was inevitable, didn't you?" He ripped open the packet and she watched him roll on the condom, her arousal building to an ache.

"Come here," she whispered, holding her arms out to him. "I want you."

"And I've always wanted you."

She heard the truth behind his words, and closed her eyes as he entered her, against the sudden tears that surprised her.

Scott was too lost in his own desire to notice, and she brushed at her eyes with the pretext of pushing away a lock of hair that had fallen into her face. She felt stripped raw, her emotions so close to the surface—grief for the time she'd wasted and joy at this moment together. She'd welcomed him into her body, but he'd breached the walls she'd erected around her heart as well.

The knowledge leant an extra intensity to their lovemaking, a depth of passion that transcended everything she'd known before. She felt closer to him than she'd ever felt to anyone, and yet free to be wholly herself. When she felt her climax building she surrendered to it fully, shouting with joy.

Scott cried out with her as he found his own release, clasping her tightly to him until their breathing had slowed and their hearts beat in a steady, strong rhythm. He withdrew, and quickly discarded the condom, but immediately pulled her close, dragging one side of the bedspread up to cover them. There, in the circle of his arms, the tears poured forth in spite of all effort to hold them back.

"What is it?" he asked, stroking her back tenderly. "What's wrong?"

"Everything," she said, her joy fast turning to misery as she contemplated the impossibleness of their situation.

"I've never known anything more right."

"It's wrong because I can't stay here," she said. She'd promised Toni—and herself—a clean break from the past. Here in Cedar Switch, as it had been in Houston, the past was like land mines hidden in her path. She'd never know when another one might explode and hurt her or her daughter. "I have to go away," she said. "I have to make a new life somewhere else."

"Then I'll go with you," he said. "I can sell real estate anywhere, you know."

She wanted to believe it would work, but she was afraid to. Lamar's death had changed everything she thought she knew about relationships. She'd thought he was a loving, devoted father and husband, yet in the courtroom he'd been revealed as a cheating drug addict with a gambling problem, who'd squandered all his money and all her trust and had ended up murdered. His actions had cost him his life and risked her own, and hurt Toni forever.

She told herself Scott wasn't like that at all,

but he'd just admitted to having a problem with drugs, and a life that was far less respectable than she would have ever guessed. Maybe he'd put that all behind him, but how could she be sure, when she'd been so wrong about Lamar?

He pulled her close once more and she surrendered, lying back and willing the tears to dry. Here in his arms she felt safer and more at ease than she had in months. For all her independence, it surprised her that she should need a man so much. Or was it only *this* man that she needed?

She didn't know how much time passed after that; she thought they might have dozed. But when a loud truck passed on the street below, Scott roused himself. "We'd better get out of here," he said, and eased away from her.

She nodded. "I need to get home to Toni." They dressed and she straightened the bedspread, not wanting to remove all evidence of their coupling so much as to preserve the room for the next couple or the next time. This would be one more memory she associated with the Palace Hotel. One more reason it shouldn't be torn down.

After making sure the coast was clear they stepped out onto the front veranda and Scott locked the door behind them. They returned in silence to his office, where he pulled her into the shadows across from her car and gave her a long, drugging kiss that made her want to plead with him to come home with her. But she didn't even want to think about explaining that to Toni, so she forced herself to push away. "Thank you for everything," she said.

"I'll see you soon," he said.

She nodded, and climbed into her car. She was giddy with the magic of newfound love—both joyful and terrified of making another mistake. Scott was a wonderful man, and he'd been wonderful to her. After all this time, she deserved happiness, didn't she? But was he the one to give it to her, or another bad choice she'd regret?

Friday morning, a large moving van pulled up to the front of the Palace Hotel and a crew of workmen began loading it with tables, chairs, beds and the other furniture that had languished inside the hotel for months. Scott, who was delivering paperwork to the title company across the street, approached one of the workers. "What's going on?" he asked.

"Everything inside's been sold to an auction company," the man said, pushing past Scott with a stack of dining room chairs.

Scott's father walked over from the court-house and joined Scott in the crowd that had gathered to watch the workmen. "Marcus must have decided to act before Marisol and her group succeed in stopping him," Jay said.

"What do you mean?" Scott asked.

"If he tears the hotel down, there won't be anything here to save."

Scott watched two workmen carry out the headboard of a bed, and the image flashed in his mind of Marisol smiling up at him, her hair spread across the pillow, her arms and legs wrapped around him. He blinked and looked at his father again. "What are their chances of stopping him?" he asked.

"Not good," Jay said. "They can try for an injunction, but as far as I know they haven't even submitted their proposal to the state historical commission. The judges around here are likely to be more sympathetic to Marcus's right to do as he sees fit with his property than with a bunch of citizens who suddenly want to save a relic that's stood vacant for more than two years."

"Could you help them find a sympathetic judge?" Scott asked.

Jay didn't answer right away. He studied his

son for a long moment. "Why would I want to do that?" he asked at last.

"Because the hotel is worth saving. As a favor to Marisol. Or as a favor to me."

"You're getting in over your head, son."

Scott looked away, not wanting to see the doubt in his father's eyes. "I don't think so," he said. "In fact, I think Marisol is just what I need. And maybe I'm what she needs." The euphoria he'd felt in the aftermath of making love to Marisol had taken a long time to fade, subsiding gradually to an underlying contentment. Yes, she said she was leaving town, but he'd meant it when he told her he'd follow her. After all the hell he'd been through he was going to find a way to work things out with her.

"If Marisol and her group want my help, I'll try to give it," Jay said. "But I'm not promising anything."

"Thanks, Dad."

"Have you spoken to Marcus lately?" Jay asked as they watched the crew begin to cart out stacks of mattresses.

"I got an offer on one of his golf course lots yesterday." He hadn't actually spoken to Marcus about it. Instead, he'd relayed the message through Marcus's secretary. "Why?"

"He called me last night at home, said he was concerned about you."

What was he, a teenager who needed reining in by his father? "What is he so concerned about?" he asked.

"He said he had heard rumors that you were involved with Marisol Luna and that given the things that came out about her late husband during her trial—concerning his involvement with drugs and gambling—he thought such an association wasn't a good idea, considering you've only been out of rehab less than a year."

"Since when is he so concerned about *my* welfare?" Scott asked. "And I resent him coming to you behind my back. What did he expect you to do?"

"He apparently thinks I have some kind of influence over you." Jay frowned.

"Look, Dad. I appreciate that you want the best for me and all. But I'm not some kid being led astray by the local femme fatale. Marisol isn't involved in drugs and never was. And I've put all that behind me now. So you can stop worrying and Marcus can shut up about it." And Scott would tell him so next time he saw him.

"I think…" Jay paused, as if weighing his words. "I think Marcus wants to know whose side you're on. He's the type of man who expects a certain loyalty from the people who work for him and the publicity Marisol has given his plans for the hotel have made him look bad—not a position he tolerates well."

"If Marcus Henry has anything to say to me, he can talk to me himself," Scott said. He turned away as the workmen carried out another bed. "I've got to go."

He walked back toward his office, fuming over Marcus Henry's arrogance. Did the man really think he could get to Scott through his father? Or that employing Scott gave him the right to dictate his personal life?

Chapter Thirteen

Scott was so caught up in these thoughts he almost didn't see the older woman hurrying toward him until she was almost upon him. "Scott," Edie Graves said, sounding a little out of breath. "I was at the library when Allison Weatherby told me something was going on over at the hotel."

"All the furnishings have been sold," he said. "It looks like Marcus Henry is getting ready to tear the place down."

"I just talked to Marisol about our plans to have the building declared a historic site," Edie said. "I've almost finished my account of the hotel's history, but we're waiting on copies of some historical photos. Damon Wright is putting together a report on the building's condition, as well."

"How much longer is that all going to take?" Scott asked.

Edie shrugged. "A few more days? Maybe as long as a week."

"By then you may be too late. I'm sorry."

Edie looked thoughtful. "Marisol doesn't strike me as a woman who gives up easily. Maybe she knows someone who can help us expedite our application."

"My father promised to look into some kind of injunction, but he didn't hold out much hope."

She shook her head. "It would be a shame to lose the old hotel."

"Until Marisol brought it up, no one else seemed very interested in saving it," he said.

"None of us with the local historical society were crazy about it being replaced by condos or whatever it is Mr. Henry plans to build there," Edie said. "But none of us was willing to take up the fight until Marisol stepped in."

"So she was the only one brave enough to stand up to Marcus Henry?"

"Sometimes it takes an outsider—or someone like Marisol, who has been away for a number of years—to wake everyone up to the possibilities of a situation," Edie said. "She's the kind of person others can't ignore."

He certainly hadn't been able to ignore her. "What will you do if Marcus tears down the hotel?" he asked.

"I've always been a realist," she said. "We may be too late to save the hotel. But there are other historic places in town that have been neglected too long. There's still time to preserve them." They said goodbye and he continued to his office. Once there, he ignored the blinking light of the answering machine and dialed Marisol's number.

"Hello?" she answered on the third ring.

"Hi. You have a minute to talk?"

"Oh, hi, Scott. What can I do for you?"

"I wondered if anyone's told you what's going on at the hotel."

"No. What's happening?"

He explained about the furniture being moved and what it probably meant. "Unless you happen to know a friendly judge who'll issue an injunction, you may not be able to stop him from tearing the place down," he said.

"I don't know any friendly judges. I feel sick."

"You did what you could," Scott said, wishing he could offer better comfort.

"If I'd kept my mouth shut, and gone about this behind the scenes, we could have had the application in before he knew what was going on," she said. "Why didn't I think of that?"

"You didn't know Marcus," he said. "You couldn't have anticipated this."

"I should have, though. I've known dozens of men like him in Houston—men used to getting their own way, who won't accept that anyone could be against them."

"What are you going to do?"

"I don't know. I have to think."

"Can I see you tonight?" he asked.

"Toni's having a friend over. I have to stay here."

"Tell her you're having a friend over, too. I'll bring dinner."

"I don't know...."

"It's just dinner," he said. "I promise to keep my hands to myself in front of your daughter. Difficult as that may be. And maybe if she gets to know me better, she'll see I'm not the big bad wolf."

She laughed, a low throaty laugh that sent heat straight to his groin. "All right. Bring pizza. I know the kids will eat that. No anchovies or mushrooms."

"Pepperoni okay?"

"Pepperoni is perfect. Now I have to go and make some phone calls."

"My dad said he'd help if he could."

"Even though he doesn't approve of the two of us seeing each other?"

"I think he's moved from disapproval to withholding judgment."

"That's something, I guess. I'd better go."

"All right. But Marisol?"

"Yes?"

"Whatever happens with the hotel, you did your best."

"I wish just once my best was good enough."

She hung up, leaving him with her words echoing in his ears. Who had her best not been good enough for? Lamar? Her mother? The people of Cedar Switch she'd known before?

He would change that. He would show her that her best, and even her second best, was more than enough for him. He knew all about falling short and falling down. Sometimes getting up was as much of a victory as crossing the finish line first.

When Scott arrived with the pizza, Toni answered the door. "Mom's not here," she said.

"Can I come in?" Scott held up the pizza box. "No sense letting the pizza get cold."

With obvious reluctance, Toni held the door open wider and let him pass. "Mom went to the store to get some Cokes," she said, following him into the kitchen. "She should be right back."

"Good." He slid the pizza into the oven and turned it on low, then faced her. "This gives you and me a chance to talk."

Toni rolled her eyes. "Don't give me any line about us getting to know each other better. I don't want to know you."

"You don't have to protect your mother from me, Toni. I'm not out to hurt her. She's been hurt too much already."

Toni's shoulders stiffened. "My mother can look after herself."

"Yes, she can. But sometimes, it's nice to not have to be so strong," he said. "To have someone to share the burden."

"Why does she even need anyone? She has me. The two of us have been doing fine."

"I don't think need is the right word." He turned a kitchen chair around and straddled it, facing her. "I know you're a smart girl, so I'm not going to talk down to you," he said. "Your mother loves you more than anything or anyone in the world. Nothing that happens will ever change that. But you will only ever be her daughter. You can't be everything else to her. Now that your father is gone, it's not unusual to think she might want another man in her life."

"My father was one of the greatest men ever. He was handsome and funny and talented and rich." Toni blinked hard, her eyes shiny with tears. "No one could ever take his place, for my mother, or for me."

"I would never presume to try to take his place," Scott said. "He was your father and I have no doubt he loved you very much. But your mother is an attractive woman with a long life ahead of her. She's suffered a lot in the past year. Do you think it's so wrong that she might fall in love with someone else? Someone who maybe isn't as great a man as your father, but someone who would pledge to love her and always be there for her?"

She scrubbed her eyes with the back of her hand. "And you think you're that person?"

"I don't know. That's for your mother to decide. Just know that I have no intention of coming between the two of you. Your relationship with your mother is special and whatever she feels for me doesn't change that."

She sniffed. "You think I'm a spoiled brat, don't you?"

"No. I think you're a young woman who's had to deal with too much change in the last year. You've lost everything you've ever known except your mother. I don't wonder you're a little possessive of her. All I ask is that you give me a chance."

She studied him a long moment, lashes half-lowered so that he couldn't read the expression in her eyes. But her shoulders relaxed, and some of the tension went out of her mouth. "All right," she said. "Just…go slow, okay? And if you hurt her, I'll come after you. Mom isn't the only one who knows how to handle a sharp pair of scissors."

Before he could respond to this bold declaration, the door opened and Marisol came in, followed by Shawna Wright. "I ran into Shawna and her mom at the store and gave her a ride over," Marisol said.

"Cool." Toni gave her mom a brief hug. "Pizza's in the oven. Shawna and I'll take ours to my room so you and Scott can talk."

Marisol sent Scott a questioning look, but said nothing until the girls had filled their plates and left them alone. "Is there something specific you and I are supposed to talk about?" she asked.

"Not really. I think that was just Toni's way

of letting you know it was okay for you to be alone with me." He slid a slice of pizza onto a plate and passed it to her. "She and I talked while you were gone. I think I convinced her I wasn't out to take you away from her or hurt either one of you in any way." He wasn't naive enough to believe he'd won the girl over completely, but she'd given him an opening, and he'd take it. With time and patience, he hoped she'd come to like and respect him, even if she never had room in her heart to truly love him.

"What did she say?" Marisol asked.

"She said I should take things slow and that if I hurt you, she'd come after me. That you weren't the only one who knew how to use a sharp pair of scissors."

Marisol choked on her soda. She set the glass down and wiped at her mouth. "She said that?"

Scott laughed. "Like mother, like daughter. I think I'd better be on my toes with both of you."

After the pizza was gone, Marisol enlisted Scott instead to help her organize all the material about the history of the hotel that Edie had brought over earlier.

She couldn't remember the last time she'd

enjoyed such a pleasant, low-key evening. They sat on opposite sides of the kitchen table with cups of fresh-brewed coffee, reading through the material Edie had compiled and occasionally commenting on some interesting fact or photograph. From time to time she looked up and watched him from behind the shield of a sheaf of papers. A thick lock of his dark-brown hair fell boyishly across his forehead, but the faint shadow of beard along his jaw reminded her he was very much a man. Her gaze lingered on his lips, and she remembered the way those lips had felt on hers—strong and sure and so focused on giving her pleasure.

And what pleasure he had given her that night at the hotel; she felt warmed through with the memory.

He shifted in his chair, and deep creases formed between his eyebrows as he frowned. "What is it?" she asked. "Did you read something upsetting?"

He shook his head, his gaze darting away from her. He dropped the papers and shoved back his chair as if to stand, but instead gripped the seat beneath his thighs, as if holding on for dear life. She realized he was breathing hard, and his skin was pale and clammy.

"Scott, what is it?" she asked, alarmed. "Are you all right? You don't look well."

"I'll be fine. Just…just give me a minute." He spoke through gritted teeth. Then he began to shake, a tremor that started in his shoulders and traveled down to where he gripped the chair.

"Should I call for help?" She headed for the telephone.

"No!"

The shout startled her. She put her hand on his shoulder. "Then tell me what I can do to help," she said softly.

"Sit down. And…and let me look at you."

"All right." She sat, and scooted her chair closer to him. She looked into his eyes, and she was startled by the anguish there. "Please tell me what's happening," she said.

"Panic attack. It'll pass in a minute." He locked his gaze to hers, his breathing harsh and uneven.

"Do you want me to bring you anything?" she asked.

He shook his head. "Just…sit with me."

She leaned over and put her hand on his thigh, and continued to gaze into his eyes, willing herself to remain calm, and to translate that calm to him. After what seemed half an hour but was more likely only five minutes, his shoulders sagged and he began to breathe more easily. He was still pale, but he no longer gripped the chair like a drowning man clinging to a life raft, and his eyes lost their desperate, hunted expression.

"Would you bring me a glass of water?" he asked.

She brought the water, and he took two pills from a bottle he pulled from his pocket. She remembered the Xanax he'd shown her before. "I'm sorry about that," he said, avoiding her gaze.

"There's nothing to be sorry about." She sat again, and kept her tone very matter-of-fact. "Does this happen very often?"

He shook his head, still not looking at her. "I can go months without having an…an attack like that. Then I might have several in a row."

"Do you know what causes it? Is it the coffee, or something I did or said?"

"No. It's nothing you did, I promise." He straightened and looked her in the eye once more. "There's no knowing what the trigger is. It could be something I ate, something I saw, not getting enough sleep the night before— no one really knows. The only thing for sure is that something in my brain, some chemical thing, perceived stress and went into overdrive." He stood and nodded to her. "Thanks for staying calm, and for not fussing or treating me like an invalid."

She rose also, and smiled. "I'm not the type to fuss."

"You aren't. That's one of the things I like about you."

She put her arms around him. "And I know you're not an invalid."

She raised her lips to his and he tightened his hold on her and kissed her with a passion that left her dizzy and breathless. There was nothing weak or frightened in this kiss. She wanted to ask him to stay with her, to follow her into her bedroom and make love to her. But of course that was out of the question with Toni in the next room. So she tried to take as much pleasure as possible from that kiss, and only reluctantly let him pull away from her at last.

"I'd better go," he said, with a look in his eyes that made her shiver and immediately crave his arms around her once more.

"I guess you'd better." She saw him to the door and stood there until his car had turned out of sight at the corner. Then she closed and locked the door and returned to the kitchen to put away the paperwork they'd sorted, reviewing everything that had just happened.

Scott's panic attack had been frightening and unexpected. When he'd told her about them before the idea had seemed so abstract. She couldn't imagine a strong man like Scott being brought to his knees by unreasonable fear.

The reality of an attack had been nothing like she'd imagined, but it wasn't his sudden weakness that impressed her most. Seeing him suffer that way and pull himself together gave her an idea of his true strength. Here was a man who understood what it was like to hurt, what it was like to have his life spin out of control.

Scott was the one person with whom she felt she didn't always have to be so strong. She could lean on him—and she could return the favor and let him lean on her. This wasn't about pity or weakness, but about trust. If Lamar had been able to be vulnerable with her that way, maybe they all could have avoided a lot of sorrow.

Hope wasn't an emotion she'd had much experience with lately, and she wasn't ready to risk hoping for anything more from the brief time she'd enjoyed with Scott. But if she took nothing else with her when she left Cedar Switch, she would take the memory of the closeness they'd shared—a precious gift like none anyone else had ever given her.

* * *

The next morning, armed with the box full of pictures and papers she and Scott had organized the night before, Marisol arrived at Marcus Henry's offices.

A very pretty redhead looked up from the front desk when Marisol entered. "May I help you?" she asked.

"Marisol Luna to see Mr. Henry," she said. She was dressed in a close-fitting red suit with a short skirt and her highest red heels. The kind of suit that dared any man to ignore her.

"I'm sorry, Mr. Henry is not in this morning," the receptionist said, not even glancing at the appointment book in front of her.

"When will he be back? I'll wait."

"I'm afraid he won't be back until next week. He left town this morning."

"He did?" Maybe this was a good sign. If Henry had business out of town, maybe he'd put off dealing with the hotel a little longer. "Would you tell him I stopped by, and that I'd like to speak to him as soon as possible?" Marisol asked.

"Of course." She took Marisol's name and number, then studied her more closely. "I saw you on TV," she said. "You're the woman who murdered that basketball player. The good-looking black guy."

"I didn't murder him. And his name was Lamar Dixon. He was my husband."

The receptionist nodded. "That's him." Her eyes narrowed. "How come you aren't in jail?"

Almost a year of practice allowed Marisol to keep her expression impassive. "Because I was found innocent."

"Guess you had a really good lawyer, huh?"

Marisol didn't bother to answer. This wasn't the first time she'd run into similar comments. Some people's brains were apparently capable of absorbing only so much information. Words like murder stuck, while a declaration of innocence barely made an impression.

"Tell Mr. Henry I stopped by," she repeated, and left the office.

She sat in her car, collecting herself and debating what to do next. The urge to drive to Scott's office and vent her frustration about Henry's absence and her theories as to what his leaving might mean was almost overpowering, but she told herself she couldn't get into the habit of turning to him.

She decided instead to visit Scott's dad. Jay had offered to help with the fight to keep the hotel, so she'd take him up on that offer.

Jay was standing in the front room of his office, talking to his secretary, when Marisol came in. "If you're looking for Scott, he just stepped out," Jay said after they exchanged hellos.

"Actually, I was looking for you," she said. "Do you have a few minutes?"

He checked his watch. "Sure. Come on back."

He held the door to his office for her, and shut it behind him. "What can I do for you?" he asked.

"Scott said you'd offered to help with the fight to prevent the old Palace Hotel from being torn down," she said. "That you might know of some legal maneuvers we could try."

"There are a few approaches we can take. We can, for instance, ask for an injunction to prevent Mr. Henry from taking any action until the State Historical Commission rules on the application to have the hotel declared a historic structure."

"Then let's do that, please."

"I can draw up the paperwork, but I have to tell you we may have difficulty finding a judge who is sympathetic to your cause."

"Let me guess. Marcus Henry has contributed heavily to every one of the local judges' campaign funds and he sends them a bottle of Scotch every Christmas. I know how the game is played, whether in a city like Houston or a small town like this one."

"Marcus Henry and his money do wield a lot of influence. But there are other factors at work."

"Such as?"

"Such as, some people see you as an outsider who's only interested in stirring up trouble."

"Would you be one of those people?" she asked.

"I know you're a more complex person than that. I know you've had a hard time and haven't always been treated fairly. But I also know you're a woman who sometimes responds to censure by flaunting the very things people most object to about you."

"I don't know what you're talking about."

"I think you do. I remember when you were accused of stabbing Harlan Davies. Before the real story came out, Harlan tried to tell everyone that you led him on, that you were an oversexed Lolita who took advantage of an older man. The fact that you were rumored to have jumped naked off the Brazos River Bridge only a few months before you were arrested only confirmed this story in people's minds."

"I didn't care what they thought of me," she said. "I knew the truth."

"And your indifference to public opinion didn't help your case. Do you remember what you said to me when I suggested if the case came to trial I should put you on the stand and have you tell your side of the story?"

She shook her head. She'd forced all thoughts of those last few months in Cedar Switch out of her mind.

"You said you shouldn't have to defend yourself when Harlan was the one in the wrong. That I should question him, not you—that no one wanted to think anything good about you, so why should you waste your breath?"

She stared at him, chilled through—not at the memory of her teenage self making this bold speech, but at the similarity of these words to the ones she'd told her defense team when they'd suggested she testify in her recent murder trial. "What does that have to do with anything now?" she asked.

"You're a difficult woman to read, Marisol. You keep people at arm's length. And now you've come to town and captured the eye of my son, about whom I care deeply."

So she'd been right all along—he didn't approve of her friendship with Scott. "Scott would be furious if he knew you were talking to me about him," she said.

"Yes he would. He has a hot temper. Also a keen sense of humor and an energy and enthusiasm that I envy. All his life, he's felt everything so keenly. Whether it's a relationship or a job or a hobby—or an addiction—he gives himself up to it one hundred percent. He's been hurt because of that. I don't want to see him hurt again."

She thought of Scott making love to her, his intense focus on the moment, the certainty in his voice when he'd told her he knew what he wanted and intended to have it. Had she ever in her life devoted so much of herself to any one thing? "You're saying the two of us are nothing alike," she said. "He's hot, I'm cold. He feels everything, while I always hold back."

"Don't use him to pass the time while you make up your mind what to do next," Jay said. "If you step in and save the hotel, then move on, it may lead to a few hard feelings, but there won't be any lasting damage. There are plenty of people who will thank you for it. But if my son gives up everything for you and you leave, it could ruin him."

She frowned. "What do you mean, give up everything for me? I haven't asked him to give up anything."

"He was dating a good, stable young woman.

The kind of woman who would have made him the perfect wife."

"I know about Tiffany. He said he didn't love her." She'd heard the truth in those words. Tiffany had been a convenience, not a conviction.

"Maybe not. Or maybe his idea of love is some great, burning passion—the kind of thing that doesn't last."

"I never asked him to leave Tiffany. I had nothing to do with that."

"Maybe not directly. And if it had ended there it wouldn't have been the worst thing in the world. Has he told you any of his history?"

"About the drug addiction and losing everything and rehab?" She nodded. "He told me." She remembered the panic attack he'd suffered last night, and the terror and pain in his eyes.

"Then you know what it took for him to come back to town and start over."

"I know." He'd been much braver than she'd been. He'd returned to Cedar Switch right away. It had taken her twenty years to face the place again.

"Months passed before he had his first client," Jay said. "Months in which he came into the office every day, ran ads in the paper, attended every Rotary Club Luncheon, Lions Club meeting and community event, shaking hands with people who talked about him behind his back, asking them to give him another chance. Little by little, he earned their trust again. He wasn't a loser meth-head embezzler, he was a local boy who'd been through hard times and come out on the other side. People began to respect him."

"And you think being seen with me is destroying that respect?" she asked, unable to keep the bitterness from her voice. "The accused murderess? The black widow?"

"The woman who drives around town in a flashy sports car, wearing a red suit that screams 'Look at me.'"

"So I'm the scarlet woman. And that's going to ruin Scott's real estate business? Are people here really so self-righteous?"

"You have a talent for making enemies whether you mean to or not," Jay said. "Men like Marcus Henry, for instance."

She made the connection then. "Marcus Henry, who employs Scott to sell his golf course lots."

"Scott received a certified letter this morning, informing him that Mr. Henry was rescinding the listing agreement," Jay said. "That's fully half of Scott's business, wiped out with one signature. And Henry has the power to see that others follow suit."

"Because of me?" She stared at him.

Jay nodded. "He left a little while ago to try to get in and see Henry."

"He's out of town. At least, that's what his receptionist says." Had Scott really lost so much of what he'd worked for because of his association with her? "What can I do to help him?" she asked.

"Leave him alone," Jay said. "Focus on your own problems and don't add to his."

She stood. "Let me know what you find out about the injunction," she said. "I'm going to meet with some other members of the committee later and see what they have to say."

"You'll think about what I've told you?"

"I will." She made the commitment even though her first instinct was to ignore everything he'd said—to defy him and Marcus Henry and everyone else who judged her harshly. If she wanted to be with Scott, she would be with him. He was a grown man. He could decide whether her company was worth everything else he might have to give up.

Chapter Fourteen

After her talk with Jay Redmond, Marisol returned to the house and searched her address book, hoping to find someone she could call on to help her save the hotel—a lawyer or politician or person with some influence. Not so long ago, she'd known many such people. She'd served with them on charitable boards, mingled with them at parties and in the private boxes at basketball games.

They had all turned their backs on her after Lamar's death. No one wanted to be associated with a possible murderess. Later, after she was acquitted, she'd attempted to contact a few of the women she'd once been close to, but they had not returned her calls. Finally, one woman had explained it would be better if they didn't see her. So many unsavory things had come out about Lamar during the trial, what with his gambling problem and the drugs and everything—Marisol understood, didn't she?

Yes, she understood. She understood that she had no one she could call on for help. Why hadn't she made more real friends? At school, she'd been an outsider, first in Cedar Switch and later in Houston. As Lamar's wife, she'd been accepted, but only as an extension of her wealthy, famous husband. There was no one in Houston who associated with her for her own sake. And truthfully, that had never bothered her before now. She hadn't felt the need to be close to others, but now that need was an aching void in her life. When she was very young, she'd fallen into the habit of keeping her distance from others to avoid being rejected, but in the end she'd hurt herself most of all.

While she was pondering this her telephone rang. "Hello?"

"Marisol? You have to get down to the hotel right away." Jessica sounded out of breath.

"What is it?" Marisol asked. "Is Marcus moving more furniture? I thought he got it all yesterday."

"He's doing more than moving furniture," Jessica said. "Damon was downtown getting lunch for his crew and he drove by there. He said there's a demolition crew there, ready to take the whole thing down."

"What?" Marisol couldn't believe what she was hearing. "Now? Today?"

"Yes. I'm going to call Edie and some of the others. Can you meet us down there?"

"Yes. Yes, I'll be right there."

She hung up the phone and thought of calling Scott, but what could he do? He had enough problems of his own, dealing with the loss of most of his business.

Downtown, she had trouble finding a parking spot close to the old hotel. It looked as if half the population of Cedar Switch had turned out to witness the excitement.

When she reached the street in front of the hotel, she saw a large crane fitted with a wrecking ball parked on the broad front lawn. A bright yellow backhoe sat beside the crane. Barricades had been set up for a block around the building, and stern-faced men in hard hats kept everyone back. Dump trucks lined a side street, waiting to carry away the debris.

"There you are!" Edie and Jessica rushed up to Marisol. Edie's hair was a mass of gray corkscrews around her head, and she wore old jeans and a man's dress shirt, as if she'd just come from cleaning house or gardening. She glared at the crane. "It certainly didn't take Henry long to set things in motion once he learned what we were up to," she said.

"I thought he was out of town," Marisol said, dazed, unable to believe what she was seeing.

"He conveniently left town," Jessica said. "But the man knows who to call to get things done."

"Can he really do this?" Marisol turned to Edie. "Can he really tear down the hotel?"

Edie looked grim. "First thing I did when Jessica called me was check with the courthouse," she said. "They say he has all the proper permits."

"Isn't there anything we can do?" Marisol asked.

"I thought about chaining myself to the backhoe," Jessica said. "But Damon said they'd just arrest me and the kids would be mortified." She glanced at Marisol. "No offense or anything."

"What? Oh." Marisol realized Jessica was referring to Marisol's arrest for murder. "That's okay."

"Knowing Marcus Henry," Edie said, "if we

chained ourselves to his equipment, he'd have one of his men hand us hard hats and they'd work around us."

"Then what are we going to do?" Marisol asked again, raising her voice to be heard over the roar of the crane and backhoe starting up.

"I don't think there's anything we can do." Edie put her arm around Marisol. "We did our best, but we didn't win this time. There are other buildings in this town worth saving. We'll do a better job with them."

A gasp rose up from the crowd as the boom of the crane swung out. Marisol cringed as the wrecking ball crashed through the side of the hotel. Glass shattered and a cloud of dust rose as a gaping hole appeared in the wall. The ball struck a second time, widening the hole, and the wall around it began to buckle. And then, almost in slow motion, the bricks slipped and collapsed, revealing a row of empty rooms, like a doll's house awaiting furnishings.

Marisol stared at those empty rooms, and felt empty herself. She'd tried so hard, but she might as well have not wasted her efforts. Why did everything always work out this way for her? She hadn't been able to repair the broken relationship with her dead mother, and Lamar had had to die before she realized how broken her marriage had been.

She'd returned to Cedar Switch hoping for something—some kind of closure or validation or something that would enable her to start over somewhere else with the confidence and strength that had all but deserted her in the long months of her imprisonment and trial. She'd settled on saving the hotel as a symbol of everything that had been good about her time in the town—the summer mornings playing there while her mother worked, and the dance recitals where she'd been a star.

And those brief moments of happiness she'd enjoyed with Scott, the man she loved. The man who loved *her* probably more than anyone ever had.

Scott! As she watched the backhoe move in to begin scooping up the wreckage and carry it to the waiting dump trucks, she thought of her conversation with his father today. According to Jay, the only thing her efforts on behalf of the hotel had accomplished was to jeopardize Scott's business and possibly even his recovery.

She turned away from the destruction of the hotel. "I can't watch any longer," she told the other women. "I'm going to leave now." She'd leave not just the hotel, but the town itself. There was nothing for her here anymore.

She was halfway to her car when a familiar voice hailed her. "Marisol!" Scott jogged up to her.

His hair was windblown, his tie loosened and the sleeves of his white shirt rolled up. A casual observer might have thought him a man without a care in the world, but the tension around his eyes and mouth proved that his outward casualness was a sham. "I've been looking for you," he said.

"I guess you saw what Marcus is doing to the hotel," she said.

"Yes. I went by his office to try to talk to him, but his secretary said he's out of town."

"I heard he canceled his contract with you." She fidgeted with her car keys, avoiding his gaze, not wanting to see blame or disappointment in his eyes. "I'm sorry," she said. "It's all my fault. This never would have happened if I hadn't pushed him on the hotel."

"It's just a contract. It doesn't matter." But his voice held little conviction.

"It does matter! I know how hard you've worked to put your business and your life back together."

He took her by the arms and turned her toward him. "I said it doesn't matter," he said. "I'll get new contracts."

She pulled away from him. "I have to go. I'm leaving town as soon as I can pack and pull Toni out of school."

"Where will you go?"

"I don't know yet. It doesn't really matter."

"I'll go with you."

"No. You have ties here. Family. You'll be better off here without me."

"You have ties here, too," he said. "You have a new business. And you have friends."

She shook her head. "All I have here is a bunch of bad memories."

"What about me?" he asked. "You have me. I love you, Marisol."

The words paralyzed her, and emotion clogged her throat. "I—I love you too," she said. "Enough to know I can't stay here and ruin your life anymore." Not waiting for his answer, she turned and ran toward her car, willing him not to follow.

Marisol's retreating car was a red blur in Scott's vision, her last words a jumble in his head. She loved him...and she thought she'd ruined his life. As if he didn't already know how to do that all by himself.

She thought it was her fault he'd lost Marcus Henry's business, but he blamed himself for being taken in by a man like Marcus in the first place. The developer hadn't been so interested in helping out a friend as he had been in finding someone he thought he could manipulate and control. Scott had gone to Marcus's office yesterday, intending to point out that Scott had a steady record of sales of the new golf course lots, despite a slow real estate market and the fact that most of the promised amenities of the development had yet to be built.

Scott saw now that Marcus didn't care about the sales as much as he valued getting his own way. He'd grown used to being the big man in this small town and had struck out at Scott not so much because of what Marisol had done, but because of what Scott hadn't done—namely, obey Marcus's orders that Scott stop seeing Marisol.

And now she was leaving him anyway. He turned and walked toward his office, his mood as black as any he'd experienced since his early days in rehab. All that effort and struggle and he wasn't any better off now than he'd been a year ago—his business was floundering, his reputation shaky and he'd lost the chance to be with the one woman he truly loved.

Some lingering self-respect chided him not to give in to self-pity. Yeah, things looked bad now, but back in rehab he'd been one mistake removed from a jail sentence for embezzlement; he'd *had* no business, floundering or otherwise; and the possibility of a woman like Marisol in his life seemed laughable.

Marisol had changed everything for him. He loved her enough that he couldn't let her walk away. Marcus Henry and the real estate contracts meant nothing. Henry thought he could ruin Scott by taking away the contract, but Scott knew from experience that outside circumstances didn't destroy a man. Only his own weaknesses could do that. And he was still strong enough to fight for Marisol.

Marisol turned her car toward home, then changed her mind and instead steered onto the highway leading to the high school. As much as Toni said she hated the place, she wouldn't mind being pulled out of class early. And she could help pack. Not that they had that much to box up. Marisol had sold or stored most of their belongings before the move to Cedar Switch.

The question now was where would they go, and what would Marisol do for a living once they got there? She'd always liked the beach, but east coast, not west. Should she try Florida? Or maybe Myrtle Beach? She had to get far enough away that her picture in the papers wasn't so fresh in people's minds. Maybe she'd cut and dye her hair, too, to make herself less recognizable.

She'd sell the car, and what valuable jewelry she had left. She'd been keeping these things back as a sort of emergency fund, but she'd need the money now to finance the move.

She'd have to cancel her dance classes. She hated to disappoint her students, but it wasn't as if they'd really had time to get attached to her. And she'd say goodbye to Jessica and Edie. She would really miss the two of them. They were her first real friends in ages. But they would understand why she had to leave.

And Scott. Leaving Scott was one of the hardest things she'd ever done, but she'd meant it when she'd said he'd be better off without her. He belonged here in Cedar Switch; she wasn't sure where she belonged.

As she turned into the drive leading up to the high school, she was surprised to see a line of buses and cars. A check of her watch confirmed it was already three o'clock. Oh, well, now she wouldn't have to check Toni out of class.

She pulled into an empty space behind a

green pickup truck and scanned the groups of students gathered around the front door. It was a startling scene—clowns, punks and cowboys mixed with a guy in football pads, someone dressed as Death, a boy in motorcycle leathers. Obviously, this was some kind of student dress-up day. Why hadn't Toni mentioned it?

Then she spotted her daughter, in the bright red and gold basketball uniform Lamar had had made for her at the start of last season. Marisol had forgotten about that uniform; Toni hadn't mentioned it since her father's death. Seeing it now brought a lump to Marisol's throat. There was so much of Lamar in Toni, in her angular frame and the regal lines of her cheeks and jaw. The uniform reminded Marisol of how close father and daughter had been. It had been hard enough for Marisol to grow up without a father she never really knew; how much more difficult it must be for Toni without the dad she had loved so much.

As Toni stood on the steps, her friend Calvin came up behind her and put his arm around her. He was wearing a suit that was on backwards, which made Marisol smile. But the smile faded as she watched her daughter with the handsome young man. They leaned close, eyes focused on each other, wrapped in that utter concentration on each other that is the hallmark of young love.

Marisol's heart ached for her daughter, who had lost so much in her short life, but was still so tender and innocent. If only Marisol could experience that again.

Toni looked up and saw Marisol's car. She said something to Calvin, who removed his arm from around her with obvious reluctance. Then Toni raced down the steps and piled into the front seat with a rush of youthful energy. "Hey, Mom," she said, tossing her backpack into the backseat, then fastening her seat belt. "What do you think of all the crazy costumes? Today was Wacky Tacky day, to celebrate the end of state testing."

"So I see." Marisol glanced at her daughter, trying hard not to appear overly curious. "I haven't seen that outfit in a while," she said. "What made you decide to wear it today?"

Toni shrugged. "I just wanted to, I guess."

"Your dad would be proud, seeing what a fine young woman you're becoming."

The smile wavered only a little. "Yeah. I hope so."

Marisol patted Toni's knee in silent sympathy. Whatever happened in the future, she and Toni would get through it together. "I have some good news for you," she said.

"What's that?" Toni flipped down the visor and checked her look in the mirror.

"You don't have to stay in school here until summer. I've decided we're moving right away."

"What?" Toni turned toward her mother, her expression filled with anxiety. "What are you talking about? Where are we going?"

"I'm not sure yet. What do you think about moving to the beach?"

"I don't want to move anywhere!" Toni wailed. "I want to stay here." She flopped back in the seat, fists pressed to her sides. "How could you do this to me, just when I've started to make friends?"

"I thought you hated it here. That's all I've heard since we got to town."

"I hated it when I didn't know anybody. It's different now."

Marisol recalled the way Toni had looked with Calvin. "Does this have anything to do with Calvin?" she asked gently.

Toni glared at her. "Calvin's a great guy. I really like him. But this isn't just about him. I like it here now. I like Cedar Switch."

"You do? You don't think it's too small? Too

country?" Both were accusations Toni had made as recently as three days ago.

"I like small. I can get to know everyone here." Her expression turned pleading. "Please don't make me have to start over somewhere else."

Marisol had prepared herself for many of the difficulties of a sudden move, but not for opposition from Toni. As she waited her turn at the four-way stop leading onto the highway in front of the school, she tried to think of the right argument to persuade her daughter that leaving town was right for them. "I know you've had a hard time here," she said. "But it will be better in a new place. We'll find a bigger school, one more like your old one. And we'll leave Texas, so you won't have all the publicity surrounding your father's death and my trial hanging over you."

"I like it that people here know who my dad was," Toni said. "That was one of the best things about wearing this uniform today—hearing what people remembered about him, and sharing my memories."

"You'll always have those memories." Marisol pulled the Corvette into the flow of traffic. "No one can take them from you."

"But you're trying to take away everything

else. Why do we have to leave now? So suddenly?"

"I realized it's time, that's all."

"What aren't you telling me? I thought you were all settled down here. Your dance school is going good. And Scott's in love with you." Her voice grew quieter. "I thought you might love him, too."

To Marisol's embarrassment, she blushed. "Why would you think that?" she asked, her voice unnaturally thin and high.

"Mom, I'm not blind. I've seen the way you two look at each other."

She watched Toni out of the corner of her eye. "That wouldn't upset you—the idea of me dating again?"

"If I could have any wish in the world, it would be for Daddy to be alive and for the three of us to be a family again. But I know that's not going to happen." Toni hesitated, then continued. "You're a pretty woman, and not too old. I guess it would be stranger if you didn't date. And Scott seems like an okay guy."

"It doesn't matter." Marisol shook her head. "Maybe I'll meet someone nice in our new home."

"You still haven't told me why you think we

need to leave all of a sudden. What happened? Did another reporter hassle you?"

"The old Palace Hotel was torn down today."

"That place you were trying to save?"

She nodded. "I guess the owner heard what we were up to and decided to take action."

"I'm sorry," Toni said. "I know you really cared about that old building, but that doesn't seem like a very good reason to leave town."

"I never intended to stay here long," Marisol said. "I don't really belong here. I realized that as I watched the hotel collapse. Better to leave now and not waste any more time."

"Mom, why do you always run away like this?"

The words shocked her so much, she pulled to the curb and shut off the car. "What are you talking about?" she asked. "Why would you think I'm running away?"

"Because that's what you do, isn't it? You couldn't handle staying in Houston where we knew everybody, so we came here. Except you'd already run away from here once, after that bad scene with your stepdad. And now things aren't going the way you'd planned here and you want to leave again."

"Toni, that's not true."

"If it's not, then why can't we stay here? We

have a house. You have a job and friends like Scott and Jessica. I'm finally making friends here. So what if they tore down that hotel? It's part of the past. Can't we forget about all that and think about the future?"

Marisol had spent the past year trying *not* to think about the future. The prospect was too uncertain and frightening.

They completed the drive home in silence, Toni slumped in the passenger seat staring morosely out the side window, Marisol lost in the turmoil of her own thoughts.

She pulled into the driveway and shut off the engine, then sat, staring straight ahead, trying to summon the strength to go inside and begin the work that needed to be done.

"What's Scott doing here?" Toni asked.

"Scott?" Marisol followed her daughter's gaze toward the front porch. A familiar masculine silhouette stood beside the door.

Marisol followed Toni up the walk to the door. "See if you can talk her out of this stupid idea," Toni said, and disappeared into the house.

"I have things to do," Marisol said. She tried to move past him, but he stepped in front of her, blocking the door.

"Don't go," he said. "Not now. Not ever. Stay here with me."

She didn't want to look at him, but she couldn't help herself. The mix of tenderness and determination in his eyes made her weak and uncertain. "Scott, I can't stay here," she said. "I tried, but it's too hard. There are too many memories—"

"Don't think about the past." He took her by the arms and turned her toward him. "Think about the future, about your dance students and seeing Toni grow up here, about Jessica and Edie and the other friends you'll make. Think about the two of us, loving each other and growing old together."

He painted such a seductive picture, but did she dare believe him? "I've made so many mistakes..." she began.

"You're talking to the king of mistakes," he said. "But I'm a big believer in fresh starts. In getting things right the second or third or fourth time around. Whatever it takes."

His kiss was as soft and welcome as spring rain, sending warmth and light into every cold and dark part of her. She clung to him, eyes closed and heart opening, wanting to believe in every possibility he offered. Maybe he and Toni were right. She'd wasted too much time focused on the past, when she could do nothing to change what had already happened.

"Is it because of my panic disorder?" he asked. "Did watching my meltdown at your kitchen table shake you up so much?"

"No! Never that." She put her fingers over his lips, as if to hold back any further suggestion like this. "I love you," she said. "I love everything about you."

"I love *you*," he said, with a fierceness that sent a thrill through her. "I fell in love with you the day I saw you standing up there on that bridge, so beautiful and so alone. You won't ever be alone like that again. Not while I'm here."

They kissed again, and she closed her eyes against the tears that flowed, tears of grief for time wasted and joy for all that lay ahead. After all the hard times and desperate moments, she'd finally run to the one place she belonged.

"We can make our own future," he said softly, pulling her closer still. "We'll make it up as we go along."

She nodded. "Yes." She could do this, with Scott there to help. Here in Scott's arms, she knew she was finally home.

* * * * *

Get 2 Free Books,
Plus 2 Free Gifts—
just for trying the Reader Service!

Get 2 Free Books,
Plus 2 Free Gifts—
just for trying the
Reader Service!

Get 2 Free Books,
Plus 2 Free Gifts—
just for trying the
Reader Service!

Get 2 Free Books,
Plus 2 Free Gifts—
just for trying the Reader Service!

HARLEQUIN
HEARTWARMING™

HW17R

Get 2 Free Books,
Plus 2 Free Gifts –
just for trying the Reader Service!